RED DIAMOND EYES

JASON K. CALDERWOOD

ISBN: 978-1-70705997-3

Front cover image by Jason K. Calderwood

Book design by Jason K. Calderwood

First printing November 2019

Independently published

www.JasonKCalderwood.com

For my parents,
*Who continued to love
an often wicked boy.*

Author's Note

While this is a work of fiction, this novel takes place
in what could be considered a parallel universe
similar to our own. In our real world, there is
no town of Emerald Ash in Northern Illinois but
there is a town of Sycamore in Dekalb County,
and many of the locations (but not all) featured
in this novel can be found there. Any relation to
real persons or events is purely coincidental (or
perhaps a synchronicity meant for the reader).

Beshrew your eyes,
They have o'erlook'd me and divided me,
One half of me is yours, the other half yours.

- The Merchant of Venice: Act 3, Scene 2

PROLOGUE

Marcus Smith wearily stared at the last cigarette in his pack, contemplating whether to light it up or wait a little longer. *Maybe not just yet,* he decided, *there's still time.*

Sitting on a dusty hardwood floor underneath a grime coated window, he let the pack with his final cigarette fall to the floor beside some recently burnt butts. Faint rays from the setting sun bleakly shone in through the window's filth, gently illuminating the room. Old, diamond-patterned wallpaper decorated the walls and was faded around areas where paintings and pictures once hung, and bubbled in spots and peeled away, exposing cracked drywall beneath. The oak hardwood floor he sat upon creaked whenever he shifted his weight, and was scattered with numerous nicks and scratches where furniture once stood. The air was thick with dust and mold. It had clearly gone to shit over the years, his childhood home.

Marcus swept a lock of salt-and-pepper hair out of his eyes and grimaced. A dull pain in his abdomen showed no sign of relenting anytime soon and a hastily applied bandage didn't do much to stop the bleeding, a small pool of crimson had formed by his side. *My blood is all over this place. I was born here and now I'll die here.* Marcus gazed deep into the puddle at his side and could almost feel the hardwood soaking it in, anchoring him to the long forgotten house like never before.

Was it worth it?

The question snuck into his mind and Marcus closed his eyes, reflecting. This had been it, something he'd waited his entire life for and something for which he was willing to risk everything—a job with a payout he could live the life of his dreams with. He had to try. While this wasn't the outcome he hoped for, of course it was worth trying.

Marcus remained motionless on the floor as a smile crept up his lips. He could still see them clear as day, sunlight pouring into the rarest set of diamonds on Earth, reflecting a million shades of the deepest, darkest red he ever saw. Not many men get to look upon a true red diamond, let alone hold one, yet only an hour ago he held two!

"Why did *he* have to show up?" Marcus screamed to the empty room. A sudden fit of coughing hit and Marcus instinctively brought his hand to his mouth. When it passed he looked at his palm, caked with dry blood and dirt, and some fresh blood from the cough, and winced. The pain in his abdomen intensified. He felt weak. It wouldn't be long now.

It had been abandoned for a couple of years, his childhood home, so of course it was the first place he sought when things started to go wrong, and of course things would go wrong, they always did. In his profession you always come hoping for the best but plan for the worst, and today was no exception. The sun rose as it always did to start the day, and was now sinking into the horizon. When it began he'd hoped to be far away by now, dreaming of ways to spend his newfound wealth. Instead he sat here, dying. It was alright though, that was the way the world worked. Some days you were lucky. Some days you weren't.

Sighing, Marcus reached down and feebly picked up the pack he'd let fall. Maybe it was luck that the job took place so close to where he grew up as a kid. Maybe it was luck that allowed him to accomplish a few things today he could be proud of, under grim conditions, wounded as he was. After all, he did complete the job (sort of) and now they were hidden, well hidden!

A car driving down the old dirt road leading to the house could be heard, sending a jolt of joy that briefly overcame the misery. A few cars had already come and gone but each time one passed it peaked his attention. The crunch of wheels on gravel grew louder as the car drew near, and trickled to a slow pace when just outside the house. Actually, there were two cars Marcus noted, as one came to a stop shortly after the other.

Could this be them? Marcus had been warned that the owners of the diamonds had a way of tracking them using a psychic or medium who could sense their general direction and proximity. He was initially skeptical but not one to take warnings lightly. Now, after holding them in his own hands, he felt an inexplicable connection to the diamonds and could also feel their presence nearby. He didn't understand it but couldn't deny what his own senses were telling him. These diamonds were truly something remarkable, perhaps even otherworldly.

Marcus flicked the lid of his pack open with the index finger of his left hand and brought the pack to his mouth. With his lips, he grabbed on to his last cigarette and let the empty pack slip through his fingers and fall to the floor. He reached in his pocket and pulled out a lighter. With difficulty, he managed to spark a flame and lit his cigarette. Outside, he heard car doors open then slam shut followed by footsteps shuffling around.

He remained silent, exhaling smoke that drifted through yellow teeth, past a crooked angular nose, and into red, watering eyes. Not bothering to pull the cigarette from his lips, he continued taking drags with the cherry glowing in front of his eyes and ash falling on his chest. After a few puffs he brushed his right hand over an object on the ground next to him, then wrapped his fingers weakly around the hilt and picked it up. It took more effort than he anticipated, lifting the cold steel off the ground, but he was able to hold on and rest it in his lap, finger cradling the cold trigger.

"Fuck you," whispered Marcus to those outside, knowing

they couldn't hear him but feeling the need to say something as he eagerly waited. He knew he was going to die and accepted his fate, accepted it a long time ago. When you're in the line of work he was a day like today was inevitable. It's just a matter of when. Now he just felt like taking a few others with him to the grave.

Still, a surge of envy washed over him for those who would still live. The rest of the world would wake up tomorrow and carry on with their lives. Would he somehow wake up and find the events of this day had just been a bad dream? Not likely. Would they find what he took painstaking steps to hide? Not likely either, but the thought of the diamonds falling back into the hands of those outside was almost too much to bear. *THEY BELONG TO ME NOW!*

Suddenly, he heard a creak from the porch as one of the men outside put his weight on the first step. *At last, one of them grew some balls. Just in time!* Marcus held on to the gun more firmly, seeming to find the last of his strength. More ash fell to his chest as he took another drag.

Footsteps followed each other slowly up the creaky wooden porch leading to the front door. He was in a room left of the entrance and wouldn't be seen when they opened the door, but as soon as they stepped in, he would be on them. Whispering could be heard as another person ascended the old wooden stairs and approached the front door.

Marcus didn't bother locking the door. All the person had to do was turn the handle and give a little shove and the door would glide open. It was kind of remarkable, he recalled, how easily the door had opened after all these years while the rest of the house had decayed around it. It was as if the house wanted him to enter, and welcomed him home. *Welcome our friends home,* Marcus thought, *let them rest here with us forever.* He raised the gun from his lap as he heard the faint metallic creak of the door handle turning. Suddenly, the door flew open.

Two men rushed in with gun's drawn, one looking to the room on the right, one to the room on the left. The man looking left had just enough time to widen his eyes in terror before shots rang out. Marcus was able to squeeze the trigger twice—with the first round finding its target, the second missing—before the other man swung around and fired, unloading three rounds into his chest. Marcus's arm dropped, the gun slipped from his fingers. Two more men stormed in.

Marcus closed his eyes...

...And tried taking a breath but his lungs sucked in a warm, thick liquid and began to burn. His body started convulsing. A voice cursed loudly. Another could be heard securing the rest of the first floor.

He opened his eyes...

...The man that shot him was crouched above a body on the floor, fingers checking for a pulse. The body lay facing him, lifeless blue eyes staring back into his, blood trickling down between curls of black hair from a hole in his forehead. Looking back up, Marcus' eyes locked with the other man whose fury at him was obvious, and who stood and approached while aiming a silenced .22 at his head.

Marcus closed his eyes...

...And saw them gleaming in his mind, clear as day. Nothing was more beautiful! A dark mass swirled in the center of each giving the impression they were pupils that bore into him, looking straight into his soul, and he could only stare back in reverence. An awesome power seemed to emanate from the diamonds and began to encompass and consume him. A terrible burning engulfed his body from head to toe, though at the same time, it was as if his physical body didn't matter anymore. Marcus felt his soul merging with something divine. A smile spread across his lips, he began to chuckle but blood spurted out instead, convulsions shook him, and all the while—till his last remaining breath—Marcus Smith saw nothing but red.

Part I

WAXING GIBBOUS

CHAPTER 1

Finisher

T he obnoxious, steady banging of a creaky bed against an apartment wall abruptly ceased as Vic Abelson stopped, mid-thrust, to reach over and check his cell phone that started buzzing on the nightstand.

"No baby, don't stop," said his girlfriend Shelly, breathlessly, fingers still digging into his shoulders.

He frowned as he read the number on-screen, this was not a call he could refuse to answer right now. "I need to take this," replied Vic apologetically, slipping out of bed and wiping away sweat that dripped from the side of his youthful, narrow face. He answered, placing the phone by his ear, his toned-muscular body naked by the side of the bed, dark skin glistening in the soft light of a candle flickering on the nightstand.

"Yeah."

"Vic, it's Dean," said a deep, authoritative voice. "Hope I'm not interrupting anything. Time is of the essence so I'll make this quick. I got a special job I think you'd be good for, a very unique situation I'm afraid. A recent job of mine didn't go exactly as planned, a fellow associate can fill you in on the details when you get there. Juicy share, biggest you've gotten yet. If you're interested that is?"

"Absolutely," replied Vic without hesitation, grin forming at the edge of his lips. This was the call he had been waiting a long time for, the last job he did for Dean was almost six months ago. Cash was tight, times being what they were, and he was beginning to worry he might have to find a *real* job soon.

"Great, that's what I was hoping to hear," stated Dean with more enthusiasm in his elderly voice. "You haven't let me down yet and I need you to come through for me on this one. There's a town in Northern Illinois called Emerald Ash, near DeKalb. There you'll find a motel called the Main Street Inn, on State Street ironically. Knock on door 113 and my man Jones will fill you in on the rest. Can you be there tomorrow?"

"Yeah, that's not a problem," replied Vic casually. Living in an apartment on the Northside of Chicago Vic knew he could make it out there quickly.

"Excellent. Make no mistake, this one's not going to be easy. I lost a good friend on this already, gonna need your full resourcefulness on this job. You helped finish another job of mine before and I need you to do that again. Don't let me down kid." Vic heard a click as the call ended. The grin on his lips grew into a full on smile. Dean had never complimented him like that before, subtle as it was, and it was pleasing to hear he was making a name for himself though Vic caught a sadness in Dean's voice that he had never heard before and the comment about losing a good friend was a little distressing. *Juicy share, biggest you've gotten yet. Those* words hung in his mind.

Shelly had been eyeing him throughout the conversation, appearing to notice his mirth. Mischievously, she smiled and threw away the covers exposing her slender naked body and gently began touching herself. With praise and the promise of wealth fresh in mind, Vic Abelson climbed back into bed with renewed vigor.

A little while later the two sat on the couch in his living room, huddled under a blanket watching television in the late hours of the night with the glow from Vic's recently acquired 4K OLED screen providing the only illumination in the small room.   Shelly's arm wrapped loosely around Vic's waist, her head lay on his chest as they watched a show about a group investigating an old abandoned sanitarium, looking for ghosts. They carried around night-vision cameras, digital voice recorders, and other weird devices attempting to catch evidence of the paranormal.

"This stuff is bullshit. Why do you watch it?" asked Vic, growing bored of watching them walk around, asking pointless questions in the dark.

"Because, it makes me scared," replied Shelly pragmatically. "I like being scared sometimes, there's a certain thrill to it." She had a thin jaw with high cheek bones that accentuated her beautiful dark eyes, which looked up into his with a playful twinkle to them. She started tickling him. "Why, does my big strong man not believe in ghosts?"

Vic twitched and gave a chuckle as she hit that one spot that she always seems to be able to find on his side. He tickled her back. "Well, I haven't personally witnessed anything paranormal but I am open to suggestion."

"Good, keep watching and maybe you'll change your mind," she replied. They gave up trying to tickle each other and settled on a long kiss before turning their attention back to the show.

"So what was that call about?" asked Shelly after a while.

Vic let out a sigh before responding. He had been anticipating this question and wasn't looking forward to having to reply. "I got a job opportunity and will be out of town for a while. I need to leave tomorrow."

"Really?" replied Shelly, sitting up. "You haven't worked an hour since I've known you. What type of work is it? I'm intrigued."

Vic hesitated, he started seeing Shelly shortly after his last job with Dean and had never gotten around to telling her how he *really* made a living. He just told her he was on unemployment and had some money saved up from before. Since he was growing very fond of her, he felt like he should tell her— he really wanted to tell her, but now didn't seem like the right time. After all, explaining that you're a professional thief isn't the easiest occupational discussion to have with a girlfriend.

"A friend of mine has a moving company and needs help from time to time. I help load and unload the truck," replied Vic. "He pays me in cash. Only problem is this move is pretty far, I might be gone about a week."

"Oh," replied Shelly, sounding disappointed. "A week, huh. Well, I'm glad we were able to spend tonight together before you go."

Vic kissed her forehead. "Me too."

Shelly lowered her head back on his chest and they continued watching television in silence for a while, eventually falling asleep in each other's arms.

Morning came quickly and Vic woke to the smell of coffee, eggs, and bacon cooking as he groggily sat up in the couch and saw Shelly preparing breakfast in the small kitchenette off the living room. Resisting the urge to lay his head back down and close heavy eyelids, Vic rose with a yawn then gave a long stretch. Figuring he had only gotten maybe three good hours of sleep, he walked a not-so-straight line for the coffee, only to find that it was still brewing. His bladder was on the verge of bursting, but he decided to give Shelly a long good morning kiss first.

"Mmm, good morning to you too," she said while flipping bacon over. Vic smiled then headed to the bathroom.

The coffee finished brewing by the time he came back and he poured himself a large cup, adding a generous helping of sugar for sweetness. It burned his mouth a little, but the coffee seemed to perk him up right after the first sip.

"Thanks for breakfast," said Vic, head starting to clear.

"No problem," replied Shelly, "I thought we could both use a good breakfast after last night. Not sure the next time you will get a good home cooked meal either, being on the road."

"I don't get many home cooked meals when working for Dean," admitted Vic. "But we do usually stop at some nice restaurants along the way."

"Well, I'm sure they don't make eggs like I do, try these," she stated as she filled up a plate with eggs, bacon, and hash browns while also filling up a plate for herself.

They sat down and ate in relative silence. Vic wolfed down the breakfast quickly and complimented her on its taste, there was something about her eggs that made the flavor unique but Shelly wouldn't divulge her secret recipe. Afterwards, they helped clean up together and ran the dishwasher.

"I need to get to work," said Shelly, checking the clock on the wall. "I'll be late as it is."

"Oh," said Vic, giving her his puppy dog eyes, "I was hoping you might be able to stay a little longer, get a little more *quality* time in."

She seemed to contemplate it for a second before responding. "Sorry babe, I can't be too late today, I have an early meeting. You're just gonna have to wait a week. Maybe I'll text you some pics to keep you company on the road," she said, flashing her mischievous smile.

"I'll look forward to that, and I'll miss you." replied Vic before giving her a long kiss goodbye.

"I'll miss you too," replied Shelly. "Call me if you get a chance to some night."

"I will."

"Oh, and one more thing," said Shelly, reaching into her purse. She pulled out a silver rosary on a beaded silver chain and handed it Vic.

"What's this for?" he asked, taking the necklace from her

and looking it over.

"It was my grandmother's, I keep it as a good luck charm," replied Shelly, looking at him with concern. "She gave it to me when I left for college and I want you to have it since you will be on the road a lot. I don't want anything to happen to you. It'll make me feel better."

Vic nodded and put the necklace in his pocket. "Alright sweetie. I'll keep it on me."

Shelly smiled and continued to stare a while into his eyes without saying anything.

Vic started to feel uncertain, "What is it?"

"Nothing," Shelly began while smiling, "I just like looking into your eyes."

Vic gave her another kiss. "And I like looking into yours. Don't worry, this week will fly by and we'll see each other soon."

"I know, see you later," she replied and headed out of the apartment.

"Bye," replied Vic, smiling as she left. He watched her walk down the hallway and around the corner before he finally closed the apartment door. Vic breathed deep, taking in Shelly's scent that remained by the door, the perfume she wore was intoxicating. He stood there for a while, reflecting, before he mustered up the energy to get ready.

A cold shower helped wake him further. Afterwards, Vic started getting his things together. He assumed he was going to need his usual items: twin silenced Glock Gen 4's with dual under-arm holsters which he hid in a special case in the closet, a belt of ammo clips, his specially crafted lock-picking set, a secure laptop, a mobile Wi-Fi hotspot device, digital encrypted-link radios, flashlights, black leather driving gloves, clothes and toiletries for the week, and the lucky white fleece he had worn on the last two jobs he worked.

It was shortly after ten in the morning when Vic left his Northside apartment carrying a large black duffle bag and entered the elevator that took him—along with an elderly neighbor who kept giving Vic and his black bag awkward glances—

to the underground parking garage. There he proceeded to his work car, a rusty brown '85 Old's that he had specially rigged for these types of jobs. It might not look like much but this car already saved his ass twice. Vic gave the tires and engine compartment a thorough inspection before starting her up. The engine purred and after letting her warm up for a while, Vic pulled out of the garage.

Traffic was light and Vic was able to hop on the Kennedy going westbound in no time. It was a bright and sunny November day that was unseasonably warm and made for a pleasant drive. He kept his usual speed of ten over as he followed the winding highway under numerous bridges and overpasses, only slowing for toll-booths or when traffic backed up at certain spots, which was normal for this time of day. Old tall and weathered buildings eventually gave way to newer, more modern buildings as Vic drew further away from Chicago and began heading through the Northwest suburbs. Once he made it past Schaumburg the highway straightened out and Vic found himself speeding up to keep up with traffic. It had been a while since Vic came out this way and he forgot how much suburban drivers liked to speed and weave in and out of lanes of traffic, which was fine with Vic as they drew police attention away from himself.

Vic was making good time and before long he pulled out his smartphone to check the roadmap and see where he needed to exit the highway, deciding to get off on a small county road going south. From there, he proceeded down a two-lane highway with countless acres of farmland surrounding him which he followed for a few miles before making a right turn heading west. He followed this two-lane highway for about fifteen minutes until he hit the county road that led into Emerald Ash.

The sun was high in a near cloudless sky as Vic passed a sign that greeted him as he entered the town that read WEL-COME TO EMERALD ASH. This was immediately followed by a couple of historic Victorian homes that were impressive to look upon on his right hand side. One appeared to be made of red brick while the other had wooden siding painted a pale beige. After passing those homes he came up to a large three story building, also on his right, and came to a stop at a red light which he was pleased to see just happened to be State Street. Vic glanced back at the building to his right, seeing four large Corinthian style columns rising from a base in the center of the building to an architrave at the top of the third floor. Atop the architrave was an engraved frieze and, atop that, a lavishly sculpted pediment, all traditional Grecian architecture Vic had learned to appreciate from a course in college. Vic was able to make out the words on the engraved frieze—DEKALB COUNTY COURTHOUSE.

A horn suddenly blew behind Vic making him realize the light had turned green and he quickly made a right onto State Street, not really sure if it was the correct direction to the motel. He passed the courthouse, noting that there was also a sculpture in front that rose about as high as the three story building that appeared to be a memorial of some sort, and came upon the main street area of town with many small businesses on each side of the road, and a good number of people on the sidewalks. Vic continued on past residential homes and once he started seeing acres of cornfields realized he probably should have made a left back at the light and turned around at Five Points Road, eventually making his way back to the courthouse then proceeding further east down State Street until he finally saw a sign for the Main Street Inn on the outskirts of town.

"Finally," said Vic as he parked in an open spot in the middle of the lot. He shut his car off and got out. All the rooms had entrances that faced the parking lot so he quickly spotted room 113 which had a DO NOT DISTURB sign hanging from the door handle. Hesitantly, Vic approached and gave a loud knock. After waiting uncomfortably a few moments he heard a latch slide and dead-bolt unlock. Slowly, the door opened revealing a stout man in his late forties early fifties who was a little shorter than Vic and had pale white skin. A brownish blotch covered a small part of his right forehead and he was almost entirely bald except for short, almost buzzed grey hair on his sides with a salt-and-pepper facial beard of the same length. A jagged scar ran from above his left cheekbone down to just above his lip, giving an even more unfriendly appearance, if that was at all possible.

"You Jones?" asked Vic.

"Yeah," replied Jones, his cold brown eyes staring into Vic's without any noticeable kindness before looking him over. After an uncomfortably long pause, he opened the door further. "Come on in."

Vic entered and an uncouth odor filled his nose of a man who had been holed up in small room for a number of days and hadn't bathed. Worn clothes were strewn about the room and a box of pizza, along with some take-out food bags, littered the floor. Vic suddenly wasn't looking forward to working with this man.

"You know why you're here?" asked Jones, motioning him to have a seat.

Vic looked to the chair Jones gestured to, a pair of pants and briefs, which hadn't appeared to have been laundered anytime recently, already occupied it. Vic picked them up and flung them to the floor in one quick flick then sat down, trying not to appear repulsed. "To finish a job. Dean said you'd fill me in on the details."

Jones laughed then, finally breaking from his stone cold gaze. "Shit, I thought that might be the case." His voice was rough, like that of a person who spent his years chain-smoking, but he moved with the ease of someone not bothered by any pains of the body and cleared a space for himself on the bed and sat down. "You look a little young. How many jobs have you done?"

"Five," replied Vic, starting to feel the slightest bit better that Jones seemed to be warming up to him.

"Alright," Jones muttered with a nod, "Dean said you haven't let him down yet. Now is *not* the time to start." Jones' eyes were constantly on Vic as he spoke, leaving the impression he was being judged the entire time. "Have you ever heard of the

Red Diamond Eyes?"

Vic thought about it a second, "No."

"Hmm, thought that might be the case too. Well your first task is to check into this shit-hole of a motel, I'm not sharing a room." Vic wholeheartedly agreed with that. "Second, see if you can find anything out about the Red Diamond Eyes, along with any recent news stories about this shit-hole of a town, then come talk to me." Jones smirked, revealing an unpleasant display of stained, crooked teeth.

"Will do." replied Vic, doing his best to conceal his unease. He checked the time on his smartphone, it was only twelve-thirty. "Meet back up around three o'clock?"

"Hmm," Jones grunted with a nod that Vic took as yes. Vic nodded back and left, glad to take in a deep breath of fresh air once he was outside. He walked down to the motel office and did as Jones instructed, getting a room a few doors down from Jones'.

Vic's room was similar to Jones' but with a much more pleasant, if slightly musky—like it hadn't been used in a while—smell. He gently laid his duffel bag on the bed and brought out his laptop and mobile hotspot, figuring he'd use his own secure internet connection instead of the free Wi-Fi the inn offered. He powered it on and did a general search for RED DIAMOND EYES which brought up some word matches, but nothing that looked like a relevant hit. Instead, Vic searched for recent news on Emerald Ash, IL and found many hits of a recent homicide nearby. He clicked on one of the stories.

LOCAL HOMICIDE STUNS COMMUNITY

Emerald Ash, IL – On the afternoon of Wednesday, October 20th, at approx. 4:40 p.m. police responded to reports of gunshots fired in an abandoned property on Old Forks Rd. where they discovered the body of Marcus Smith, who was pronounced dead at the scene from numerous gunshot wounds. Witnesses reported two vehicles speeding away shortly before police arrived. An active investigation is currently ongoing. Any witnesses or anyone who may have relevant information on the case are asked to come forward and call the Emerald Ash police at 815-555-9796.

Vic continued to read similar reports though none really offered up any further info than what he had already read. No suspects. No motive. No mention of these diamond eyes Jones spoke of. He read every article he could find on the subject but the only additional details he could find were that county coroners determined the death was caused by gunshot trauma which was ruled a homicide and police are actively investigating. Vic went back to searching for variances on red, diamond, and eyes but didn't seem to be finding anything relevant after searching for an hour.

It was right at three o'clock when Vic left his room to check back in with Jones, something he wasn't entirely looking forward to. A knock on room 113 went unanswered, and after knocking a second and third time, Vic gave up and went back to his room feeling a bit apprehensive that Jones didn't answer. He decided to leave a note with his room number and went back and slid it under the door to Jones' room, noting the DO NOT DISTURB sign still hung there untouched.

Vic returned to his room, realizing the lack of sleep from the night before was starting to catch up with him. His stomach rumbled, the breakfast Shelly cooked for him seemed like an eternity ago so he grabbed the phone book off the desk and leafed through the pages looking for places that delivered, eventually settling on a burger, fries, and mozzarella sticks. With nothing to do till he heard back from Jones, Vic laid down on the bed and turned on the television. His food was delivered a short time later, and it was well after eight when Jones finally knocked on his door.

"Sorry, I dozed off," said Jones nonchalantly as he walked in. "So, you find out why we're here now?" He grabbed a leftover mozzarella stick Vic had on his table open and shoved the whole thing in his mouth. There was still a noticeable odor emanating from him though it seemed better than before.

"I didn't find out much about the Red Diamond Eyes, but I have an idea of what we're doing here," replied Vic. "I'm assuming this has to do with some diamonds, or something known as the Red Diamond Eyes, and the unsolved homicide of one Marcus Smith."

Jones nodded while chewing and swallowed some before speaking. "Yeah, that's right. Marcus was a good friend of Dean's. He was on a job of his." Jones swallowed the rest of what was in his mouth. He stared at Vic and his eyes narrowed and his brow creased. "Shit went bad, there wasn't supposed to be anyone home but after Marcus secured the target and was on his way out he got tagged by a bodyguard, some stupid security detail that wasn't supposed to be there, got shot in the abdomen but managed to get away." Jones grabbed a couple fries and chewed thoughtfully.

Vic nodded, "That lines up with the injuries I read about Marcus. Didn't mention anything about a robbery though, or any recovered items."

Jones grunted and continued chewing, and looked like he was about to reply but instead sat down in a chair next to the food bag, not finding anything left. He swallowed and turned his attention back to Vic. "Not in any news article I read either. Cops certainly haven't figured out what Marcus was doing in that house. Dean wasn't even too sure, at first. Now we think it's safe to say that Marcus stashed the target somewhere in that house. Now it's up to us to find it."

"And what exactly is our target?" asked Vic, beginning to feel uneasy about accepting this job.

Jones just smiled and grunted in a way that unsettled Vic even more before finally answering. "The Red Diamond Eyes."

Vic frowned and noticed that Jones seemed to be taking a slight pleasure at his unease in being left in the dark.

"Tomorrow morning at seven sharp, we'll go on a little reconnaissance mission, and I'll tell you all about them," Jones said as he got up from the chair. "Until then, do a little more research. See if you can find *anything* about them. Might be a little easier to accept what I have to say about them if you read it from an outside source first. Maybe see if you can find anything out about the house Marcus was found in as well."

"Alright," replied Vic, not feeling any better about the situation.

Jones nodded and left. Vic set his alarm—before he forgot to—so he was sure to wake up in time then quickly went back to his computer, seeing if he could have any better luck searching. It was a little after eight-fifteen and Vic wanted to make sure he had time to get a good night's rest in, though he worked well into the night searching, and fell asleep with the laptop next to him on the bed.

Vic's alarm clock rudely woke him up from a pleasant dream he couldn't fully remember right at six in the morning. Being unemployed and lazy, he had gotten in the habit of sleeping in late so he naturally felt like shit at this hour. He used the small coffee brewer the motel provided, along with a very stale looking single serving packet from some brand he never heard of, to brew a cup of coffee that ended up tasting horribly bitter and acidic, but it did help clear his mind and bring him back to life. A cold shower later and Vic was as ready for the day as he could be, and was a little surprised when Jones actually knocked on his door promptly at seven.

"We'll take your car," said Jones, not leaving room for argument. "This is just a little drive we are going on so make sure you don't have anything stupid on you. We're just visitors from out of town on this trip."

"Well in that case," Vic took off his jacket and slid the holster that held his Glock's off and placed them back in his duffle bag. Then he put his coat back on and grabbed the DO NOT DISTURB sign from the back of the door as they left and placed it on the handle outside.

Vic led Jones to his 'Olds in the parking lot. They got in and Vic started her up and let the car warm up for a bit before pulling out onto State Street heading west, he at least did enough research last night to figure out how to get to Old Forks Road from the motel. They drove down State Street in silence, passing the courthouse, downtown Emerald Ash, and Five Points Road.

"You know how to get there?" asked Jones as they drove further through the outskirts of town.

"Yeah, I should be good," replied Vic. "But let me know if it looks like I'm going the wrong way." Jones just grunted which Vic was starting to view as a common reply.

It was about seven-thirty when Vic pulled off onto the narrow grass shoulder of Old Forks Road, after successfully finding it, and put the Old's into park. They saw it in the distance— their job. It stood atop an old crumbling foundation, two stories tall. Wood panel siding, which still had sporadic flecks of white paint that somehow clung to it, were heavily worn and weathered down to a rusty gray brown. Sickly green shingles rose up a steeply sloped roof that looked like it was about to cave in. A small porch with an overhang that protruded from under two second story windows led to the front door of the house. On the other side, at about the same level as the front, was an overhanging roof that connected to what may have once been a porch, but now was nothing. Its posts hung above the ground, dangling from the corners of a roof that connected to the house just under the second story windows facing the back of the property, and which hung precariously to the side of the house. All visible windows and doors were boarded up, leaving no easy access in. An old barn stood about twenty feet behind the house and appeared to be in worse shape than the house itself. It was not a welcoming sight. They watched the house in silence for a minute before Jones spoke up.

"So, you do your homework last night?" he asked, sounding more focused than Vic heard before. "Any ideas on how to get in?"

Vic continued to look at the house as he responded, "Yeah, the cops boarded up the doors and windows shortly after the incident but I was able to find a forum online where some local teenagers were bragging about how they busted in and partied inside." Vic pointed toward the back of the house, with the overhang that connected to the porch-that-wasn't. "On the back of the house, facing that barn out there, is a recess that leads to an emergency escape window in the basement."

Jones looked to where Vic was pointing and grunted while nodding, Vic got the impression he liked what he was hearing so far.

"Those kids were saying the boarding to that window is loose. It should pry open easily and then we could pop it back in place when we're in."

Jones looked over at him, questioningly, "How'd you find this forum, Google?"

Vic laughed, figuring that based on Jones' age he probably wasn't the best with newer technology. "No man, Google's search results are largely ad-driven, and aren't really good at highlighting things like this. A friend of mine is a hacker and gave me a special program that ignores all the advertised bullshit and returns much more relevant hits. It may take a little longer to search for things but I get way more accurate results than sites like Google or Yahoo."

"Any risk of searches or shit getting traced back to you?"

"Not really. I use a mobile hotspot that's not in my name along with a VPN proxy. About as anonymous as you can get these days. That forum I mentioned was a public forum anyway, anyone can access it. Those kids are fucking stupid for bragging about their criminal escapades on the internet. Cops can prosecute now based on seemingly random comments people post on their friend's social media, thinking no one else will give a shit. It's not really a safe place for information like that. Plus you never know what devious asshole may be lurking about, gathering information on you and your activities." That drew a laugh from Jones.

"So what do we do when we're inside?" asked Vic.

"I have some gadgets of my own," said Jones, casually. "I did a little inspection on this place before you got here. Once we get in I'm planning on drilling little holes through the boarding of each window on the second floor and putting cameras in. They're about the size of a pen so they won't be noticeable from the outside, especially at night which is when we'll go in. These will link into my laptop which will be a command center of sorts. We'll have eyes on the outside even though these windows are boarded up and I have software that will give off an alarm if motion is captured by one of the cameras. That way one of us doesn't have to spend the night watching the screen. Once that's setup, then we get what we came for and get the fuck out."

Vic was impressed, Jones did know a thing or two about new technology, and after hearing his thoughts was starting to feel a little better about accepting this job. There were only a few questions remaining, and one big one came to mind. "So what exactly is it we're looking for? What are the Red Diamond Eyes? I couldn't find *anything* on them last night."

Jones sighed and gave Vic a worried look. "Well, they're essentially what the name implies—a matching pair of red diamonds that people call the Red Diamond Eyes. But there's a little more to 'em than that." Jones' eyes locked with Vic's inquisitively, "Do you believe in the supernatural?"

Vic's brow creased at the odd question. "The supernatural, huh. Well, my girlfriend likes watching shows about ghost hunting and is into that sort of thing. I'm still a little undecided on all that but I try to be open-minded. And are these diamonds really *red*?"

Jones nodded. "Yeah, deep red and very rare. I not gonna lie to you, Dean told me some messed up shit about them."

Vic gave an uneasy laugh, "Okay, like what?"

"Their cursed for one, and apparently the targets they were stolen from have some sort of psychic or medium that's able to sense the diamonds and lead them to their general vicinity. That's how they were able to find Marcus in the house."

"Jesus," replied Vic, surprised at what Jones just unloaded on him which left him feeling unsettled and apprehensive. "Are we sure they didn't already find the diamonds? Seems like they would have a better chance at it than we do."

"We're sure," said Jones confidently. "We have an informant of sorts on their side. They still haven't gotten the diamonds back, and they're furious as hell over it. We should assume they are working on a plan to get inside and get them as well." Jones said as he scanned the area in front of them.

Vic's mind was racing, this was turning out to be the most challenging and dangerous job he's worked and every time Jones spoke it just led to more questions. "If these diamonds are so unique it sounds like they may be difficult to offload. Does Dean have a buyer for these lined up?"

"We wouldn't fucking be here if he didn't. And the buyer is willing pay full value for these two little diamonds. Genuine red diamonds like these are extremely rare and highly valuable. These two are around five and a half carats each which values them at around five million apiece, so that's ten-fucking-million dollars riding on this—riding on us!" said Jones with a gravity that really hit home for Vic. After a moment, however, the slightest crease of a smile turned up on Jones' face. "But that's also why our cut is so good, and what's gonna make this all worthwhile."

Vic's ears perked up and he looked to Jones, he'd been waiting to ask but it didn't seem right until now. "So what is our cut?"

Jones smirk turned into a full blown smile. "If we pull this off, then he gets half and we get half. Our half will then be split evenly." ← Dean

Vic was too stunned to speak for a moment but finally managed to blurt out. "Two and a half million each! That's our cut? Holy shit!" That was well over four times the payout of all the other jobs he'd done combined.

Jones cut into his moment of surprised joy, "Don't go

blushing all prettily just yet, fact is in order to get that payout we gotta do the seemingly impossible first. We gotta find those two red needles in a haystack. No diamonds, no cut for any of us."

Vic looked to the house, feeling his pulse quicken, an excitement surged through him. This is what he was meant to do, he understood it now. Whenever someone told him he couldn't do something it always seem to push him harder. Anytime he failed, he would start over until he succeeded. Vic looked at the house and a calm clarity washed over him, a concentration of will that he recognized was in him and drove him at hard times in his life to push even harder, and think more quickly and deftly than those around him. He knew what needed to be done now, he knew the stakes. He knew he needed to succeed at all costs. After all, he was a man who got things done, who finished what was started. He looked to Jones and smiled. "Well, what the fuck are we waiting for? Let's get in there."

Jones grinned back, seeming to share his excitement. "I like your enthusiasm, unfortunately, it looks like we got our very first road block," Jones nodded ahead, looking at the dirt road that stretched out before them. "You're in the driver's seat, time to see what you're made of."

Vic looked up and saw a car approaching, on top of the cabin were the unmistakable mounted lights of a police cruiser.

CHAPTER 2

Law of the Land

"Alright, I got this," said Vic, hoping he appeared confident. He was well aware of the certain way things were handled professionally, a law of thieves if you will. Vic was in the driver's seat, he was in control and was the point-man on this and Jones would follow his lead.

Vic reached under the dash feeling around, he slid aside a panel beneath the steering wheel and flipped a switch within. Satisfied, he looked to Jones who had a puzzled expression.

Jones let out a grunt, "What the hell?"

Vic grinned, "Don't worry, just giving us an alibi."

"Don't worry, right." Jones sounded doubtful while shaking his head.

The police cruiser slowed as it approached and Vic read DEKALB COUNTY SHERIFF on the side. The Sheriff's window began to roll down as his patrol car neared, Vic took the queue and began to roll his down as well. As the patrol car came to a stop, the Sheriff turned his attention to Vic, eyes hidden behind mirrored aviator sunglasses.

"Everything all right here?" asked the Sheriff, face expressionless. He had a thick dark brown mustache and a wide-brimmed hat which, along with his sunglasses, made him look like a textbook cop. Vic had dealt with plenty of these types before.

"Actually, we're having a little trouble with our car," Vic began casually as he turned the key in the ignition. The engine turned but didn't start up. "I think we just ran out of gas. We were trying to get a hold of a friend of ours but he's not answering his phone. You don't happen to have a gas can, do you?"

Vic heard Jones makes an indiscernible noise and look out the passenger window. If Jones didn't like how he was handling things, he was sure he'd hear about it later. Vic tried not to let his face betray any thoughts to the Sheriff.

"As a matter of fact, I do. I'll pull up behind you," he replied then drove forward and began making a three point turn.

"Interesting way of proceeding, but I'm not entirely opposed," said Jones.

"We'll be fine," replied Vic while cautiously eyeing the Sheriff in the rear-view mirror. He pulled the keys out of the ignition, opened the door, and stepped out of the car, walking to the rear of the 'Olds. As the Sheriff pulled up behind him, he smiled and opened the gas panel on the side of the car and began unscrewing the cap. The Sheriff put his patrol car in park and got out, leaving the cruiser running, then walked around back to the trunk.

"So, where are you from?" asked the Sheriff as he walked up, holding a two gallon gas can.

"Chicago," replied Vic. The vehicle was registered to an address downtown so he wanted to make sure his story matched in case the Sheriff ran the plates. "Thanks for your help, we really appreciate it!" Vic took the gas can and nodded in thanks, it felt nearly full.

"Just doing my duty," said the Sheriff solemnly, Vic noticed he was looking at the house but turned his head and stared back at him. "The name's Eli, DeKalb County Sheriff."

"I'm David," Vic replied without hesitation. That was the

name on the driver's license in his pocket at least. He knew the Sheriff was expecting more of a reply but he wasn't willing to venture forth any information he didn't need to so he flipped open the cap and started pouring gas in the car.

"So where you boys headed?" asked Eli, offhandedly. "You're sort of out in the middle of nowhere here."

Vic took a second to reply, hoping he thought this through well enough. After all, this is where he needed to be on his game. "We're in town for a couple days with some friends," he said a little louder than normal so Jones could hear him and back him up, if needed. "We're helping them move." Not the best reply but hopefully that will snub any questions about their friends' name or address, this Sheriff seemed like the sort that may know the majority of folks under his jurisdiction, this being a small town and all.

Jones opened the door and stepped out. He eyed Vic who continued to pour the gas, but seemed calm. "Just seeing if you needed any help," he said.

"No, just thankful the Sheriff was around to lend a hand," replied Vic.

"My names Eli," the Sheriff said to Jones, reaching his hand out, "DeKalb County Sheriff."

"Paul," replied Jones as he shook the Sheriff's hand. "Appreciate the assistance."

"Anytime, always a pleasure to help those in my jurisdiction ," said Eli coolly. "I like to ensure it's a friendly, peaceful county for those who call it home."

"Well, I've enjoyed it so far," Jones replied with a smile.

"You gentlemen aware of what happened in that house over there?" asked the Sheriff, gesturing at the house with the boarded windows. "Unfortunate bit of business. Seems there's been a run of law breakers in this area recently."

Vic froze.

"No, can't say I do," replied Jones calmly. "To be honest, this genius over here made a wrong turn and we're not exactly sure where we're at." Jones had nodded to Vic who just smirked and shrugged his shoulders.

The Sheriff stared back at Jones for a second. "Well, I'm sorry to say but I'm gonna need to see your ID's," said Eli, losing his friendly edge. "Wouldn't be doing my job if I didn't ask."

"Sure, no problem Sheriff," Jones replied as he reached into his back pocket. He pulled out his wallet, took the ID out, and handed it to the Sheriff. Vic finished pouring gas and handed the gas can back to the Sheriff, then pulled his driver's license out of his pocket and handed it over.

"I'll be right back," the Sheriff stated, heading back to his patrol car. He put the gas can back and closed the trunk then walked to the driver's seat and sat down.

Vic looked to Jones, who wasn't smiling. Vic continued smiling but started to feel nervous. He knew his ID would check out, no worries there. He wasn't sure about Jones', but maybe Jones was thinking the same about his. Best to get this situation finished up quickly. They stood at the back of the car in silence while the Sheriff worked the computer inside, after a couple minutes the Sheriff got out and walked up to them, face expressionless.

"David, Paul—I don't want to see you guys by this house again," the Sheriff said flatly as he handed Jones his ID back. Jones nodded in consent.

"Understood," replied Vic as he took his ID from the Sheriff. "We owe you anything for the gas?"

"Don't think anything of it," The Sheriff replied while shaking his head. "Drive safe." He walked back to his police cruiser and got in. Vic and Jones exchanged a quick glance then got back in their car, Vic reached under the dash and flicked the switch back up, started up the car, and drove off. Vic watched in the rear view as the Sheriff's car grew smaller in the distance, staying parked on the side of the road.

The rode in silence for a while, passing acres and acres of fields that had just been harvested of corn. Farmers were out with tractors plowing and breaking up the dirt in preparation for the winter season. There were times he envied farmers.

There was a shit ton of work to do on a farm, but on days like today, tending your own land in the morning sun didn't seem like it'd be so bad. Way less stressful than how his morning was going.

"You did good back there Vic," said Jones, breaking the silence. "I wasn't sure I liked where you were going with it at first, but you held your own with the Sheriff. You're a damn good liar." He was looking at him curiously.

Vic thought Jones may have been implying that he was not be entirely up front with him on things, but Jones seemed like he was being the same way himself. "Thanks, you too. I'm glad you replied when he asked about the house, I'm not sure I would have been as casual with my reply."

"Well, as I'm sure you know, you don't get far in our profession without being an expert bullshitter," Jones grinned. "Cops are usually bound by protocol anyway, so fucking predictable."

"Unfortunately, it sounds like we aren't going to be able to go on any more joyrides by the house," said Vic. "This vehicle is now marked, I'm sure he'll be keeping an eye out for us."

Jones lost his grin and looked at him, a more serious expression on his face. "Agreed, how long had we been there for, twenty minutes?"

Vic nodded, that sounded about right.

"I'm thinking they have a patrol car come through regularly, maybe at certain points throughout the day," Jones mused. "The house is definitely being watched, that adds a certain element to this job. Add to that, the possibility of local's wanting to explore or get fucked up in an old abandoned house, along with the previous owners of the diamonds possibly staking this place out, and that makes this job *much* more challenging." Jones looked at Vic with a hint of concern on his face. "Once we're in there, things can go to shit in no time. We need to go in and do our search quickly, efficiently, and then get the fuck out as soon as possible. Due to your nice little tale about us helping friends move that puts our faces in this town for only a short period of time. Any longer than a few days and if we run into that Sheriff again, we won't get off so easily."

Vic had come to the same conclusion. Their responses worked for now but they didn't have much time. "So you finally gonna fill me in on your plan? You seem to be leaving me guessing what's next all the time." Vic came up to State Street and made a left, heading into town.

"Yeah, I'll fill you in," replied Jones. "Dean wants this done right. We finish the job and don't leave any loose ends. I have a satellite map of the area and planned out a spot where we can drive to and leave our car. Then we'll head through some farmland under the cover of night and come up to a spot behind the house, using the barn as cover. Assuming everything's clear we'll dash to the basement entry you noted. I'll need to get in and setup the cameras quickly to get our eyes on the outside operational. Once setup, we find those diamonds as quick as possible then disappear. Leave like we were never there. Now realistically that's probably not gonna happen, we might have to tear through some shit in that house if it gets to that point."

"We're gonna be in there a long time," Vic interjected. "What if the Sheriff comes snooping by the house, or some people associated with the previous owners of the diamonds?"

Jones looked at Vic, eyes cold. "Then we take of it."

Vic nodded but remained silent, turning his attention back to the road. He knew exactly what Jones meant. An uneasiness ran through Vic, while he had done five jobs for Dean and had established himself as a cunning thief, the jobs he had done might have gone a little too well. Vic carried his twin silenced Glock Gen 4's on jobs, but never actually used them. Vic had never shot or killed anyone before.

"We're going to do this tonight," stated Jones, looking forward. "We'll go over the plan in detail once we get back to the motel."

Vic wondered if Jones sensed his unease. "The sooner the better as far as I'm concerned."

They passed the courthouse and it wasn't long before Vic

pulled in the parking lot of the Main Street Inn, choosing a spot further back towards the rear and out of sight of the main road in case the Sheriff drove by. They spent the next couple hours going over the plan in Jones' room. The satellite map Jones had of the area proved to be detailed and his course well plotted out. They had quite a bit of gear they would be hauling so it wasn't going to be a fun hike. Their path led them mainly through farmland, but they would be following a creek which led close to the house and had trees and bushes that ran along its banks to use as cover and a place to hide their gear, if needed.

Jones would enter first and setup the cameras and the laptop using the master bedroom as the command center while Vic stayed outside on lookout. The cameras have motion sensing capabilities and Jones said that if someone was outside moving around the laptop would let out a buzz they should be able to hear, but shouldn't be heard outside. However, depending on where they were at in the house, they might have trouble hearing it too. Since there was no power in the house everything was dependent on batteries which should last about eight hour's total. They were going to search as long as they could and if they didn't find anything the first night pack up and try again.

Once the plans were set, they parted ways to rest up and get ready for the night. Vic had a few hours on his own, so he ordered some food, packed his things, and spent some time searching for more stories on the case. He wasn't finding any new information and didn't end up searching long. After eating he started to feel drowsy, the early morning wakeup call and little sleep he had gotten with Shelly the night before was taking its toll so he decided to lay down and get some sleep. After all, it was going to be a long night.

Vic fell asleep in no time.

He wore orange prison scrubs and shackles, fettered hands and feet with chains that ran up through a leather belt at his waist. Looking ahead he saw a progression of inmates dressed the same, shuffling forward in a single-file line that seemed to go on forever. They moved down a long dark corridor with iron bars of prison cells on either side of them, the only light coming from caged lamps with a single dim bulb that hung low from a high ceiling and were spaced a lengthy distance apart. Doors to the cells were open but he couldn't see far inside due to shadows from the spacing of the lights. Faint screams seemed to resonate around him. A fear began to surge through Vic Abelson, a fear that he had been caught doing something horrible and this was his punishment.

They slowly moved forward for what seemed like an eternity, sluggish shuffling with chains that dragged and scraped on the stone floor as they passed cell after cell. It suddenly struck him that there were no guards around, no one leading them where they needed to go. Vic looked over the shoulder of the person in front of him and could only see the line extending endlessly on with everyone facing forward. He dared to look around behind him...

And was suddenly shoved into one of the cells and fell hard on the floor as the chains kept his foot and arms from reaching out to brace his fall. The cell door slammed shut behind him. Vic rolled over onto his back, realizing it was an isolation cell with a solid metal door that closed him off from the hallway outside. A sliver of light shone in from a small square window near the top of the door. Darkness consumed him but for the light from the window that cut through the black of the cell. After cowering on the floor a while he managed to get to his feet and approach the window, standing on tip-toes while trying to peer through.

"Who's out there?" he squeaked, catching movement of some sort. An odd noise could be heard, almost indiscernible, and it seemed as if the source of light outside the cell began to move. "Why am I here?"

A sudden splash of red covered the window, startling him. Vic took a step back. A dark fluid seemed to be filling the hallway outside his door, rippling back and forth across the window as he watched. Vic looked down as the light source continued to move and reflect a wavy square pattern on his chest that turned a dark red with the fluid outside. It terrified him.

"No," whispered Vic. He took a few more steps backward, no longer caring to know why he was here, now only feeling the strong urge to hide. It continued to rise outside his cell and Vic continued to step back until he hit the wall behind him. The square window became completely enclosed with fluid and turned a deep red. The light continued to shine down on his chest. The liquid outside was blood, he realized.

"Why me?" he whispered. He began shaking. A hopelessness consumed him, an all-encompassing despair as the realization hit that he was doomed to spend the rest of his days here, locked up alone. He slid to the ground and curled up in the fetal position, shackles clenched tight, darkness hugging him—suffocating him.

The red square now illuminated the wall above him, and began creeping downwards as the light source outside the room began to shift again. Vic peered up and could only watch, paralyzed in fear, as the light crept closer towards him. A sudden beating noise startled him. It came from his cell door, two quick pounds—then silence—then another two pounds. He felt the energy of it in his chest, it seemed to shake the whole room.

"Who's there?" cried Vic. The square continued to move down the wall until it was just above his head. Another pounding rattled the cell door twice, louder this time, and Vic felt its beating in sync with his heart which felt like it was about to explode. The light source from outside the door continued to move and the square began to cover his face. Vic sheepishly looked towards the window as blinding light shone through. Two beats pounded again, and on the second beat, the door gave way and burst towards him followed by a flooding rush of blood. As it was about wash over him, Vic woke up in his bed in the motel room, curled in the fetal position. Two loud pounds startled him further and he finally realized someone was knock-ing on his motel room door.

Befuddled and with his heart still pounding, Vic got up off the bed. Rain could be heard pouring down outside and a flash of lightning lit up the window, quickly followed by the rumble of thunder. A storm was beating down. Vic walked up to the door, undid the latch, and opened it to see Jones staring back at him with rain beating down on his freshly-shaven head.

"It's time."

CHAPTER 3

Fearless

J ones frowned, looking him up and down in obvious dismay over his appearance. "You look like shit. I'll give you a couple minutes to get ready. Meet me in my car in five minutes. It's the rusty old Caddy out there." He gave another appalling look then shook his head and walked away.

Vic closed the door and took a deep breath while closing his eyes. He was back in the cell, unable to move—crippled by fear. It had been a long time since a dream disturbed him that much. A memory shot into his mind from when he was a kid, he had just woken from a nightmare, screaming. His father rushed into his room.

"What's the matter son?" asked his father, eyes filled with concern.

"I had a bad dream," Vic had said, sobbing. "I want to sleep with you and mommy tonight."

His father looked at him awhile before responding, "You had a bad dream last night and slept with us then. You can't keep doing this every night. It's not easy when you have bad dreams, trust me I know, but you need to realize that your dreams are just that—dreams. They aren't real. They can't harm you. You wanted your own room away from your sister, well now it's time you started sleeping here on your own and making it through the night."

"But I'm scared."

"Then you must learn to be fearless," his father replied.

Vic had thought about it for a moment. "How do I do that?"

"It's not entirely easy to tell you the truth," his father began gently, "because there are a lot of times when you are naturally going to feel afraid. Like right now, when you wake up from a bad dream in the middle of the night. It's dark, your mind plays tricks on you. You're afraid. But you need to realize that the first step in becoming fearless *is* to feel afraid. Then tell yourself what you just experienced was only a dream. It isn't real. There's nothing hiding in your room. Tell yourself that you're fearless! You'll find strength inside you, the fear will fade and the dark will recede. Can you be fearless for me?"

He thought about it a while. "I'll try," he said earnestly.

That night he made it through until morning without calling for his parents. There were times where he wanted to call out, when fear gripped him and darkness came crawling, but he closed his eyes, tucked the covers all the way up under his chin, and rode it out.

Vic opened his eyes, feeling silly. The rain was still pouring down and thunder rolled but there was work to do. He went to the bathroom and splashed cold water on his face then ran a comb through his short hair. After putting on deodorant, he walked out of the bathroom and grabbed his holster, which held his two pistols, and slid those around his shoulders. He put on his coat then picked up the bag that contained the rest of his gear and headed out the door.

Jones was waiting for him in the car, a beat up rusty old Cadillac with the hub caps missing. By the time he got the bags

in and was seated in the passenger seat, Vic's clothes were damp
and his hair was dripping wet.

"You good?" asked Jones, worried.

Vic knew Jones wasn't genuinely concerned about his
wellbeing but understandably concerned about his ability to
do what they had to do tonight. "Yeah man, just dozed off there.
Didn't mean to sleep that long," replied Vic, trying his best to
sound confident.

Jones nodded. "No worries, we got a long night ahead of
us. I checked the weather before I left the room," Jones said
while putting the car in reverse. "This should pass over us by
the time we reach our parking spot. Just a small thunderstorm
moving through. Another one should pass over while we're in
there which should make for a fun night."

"So much for not leaving a trace in the house, we'll be
tracking mud all over the place by the time we get there." Vic
stated.

"No man, we'll just take our shoes off when get in." Jones
quipped.

Vic laughed, Jones' mirth helped lighten the mood. Visions from his dream were still fresh in mind and he needed
something to help clear his thoughts and get him focused.

Jones backed up the Caddy and pulled out on to State
Street, going in the direction of the courthouse. They rode in silence and it seemed like almost no time at all had passed before
arriving at their destination, a row of thick bushes off an unlit
back country road. Jones guided the car off the road and behind
a row of tall bushes that concealed it well.

The rain had let up and was barely coming down as Vic
exited the Caddy and grabbed his bag. The buzzing of insects
and wildlife around them, along with the trickle of rain, made
soothing background noise, helping to further ease Vic's tension. Jones grabbed his large bag and slung it over his shoulder
then closed the trunk of the Caddy. Jones' bag looked bulky and
heavy, and left Vic wondering just what Jones had brought with.

"Follow me," said Jones. He began walking off into the

darkness.

A cold November wind blew strong and the breeze bit through his coat making Vic shiver. Once they were inside, the house would at least offer protection from the wind, but it was still going to be cold and Vic was wishing he brought a heavier coat. He put on a pair of gloves he had in his jacket, folded his arms under his chest, and followed Jones along the muddy creek which was mushy and slippery, with puddles everywhere. It didn't help that the heavy bags they carried left them unbalanced. After a couple minutes of walking Vic slid and fell on his ass. Jones just laughed at him and watched as he struggled to get back to his feet. So much for not tracking mud across the house.

Jones continued on and it wasn't long before he lost his footing on a sharp incline and fell on his hands and knees in the mud. Vic just wasn't in the mood to laugh when that happened. Jones got back up, muttering angrily under his breath. They made their way slowly and carefully after that, following the course of a winding creek that divided acres of farmland.

The rain ended and clouds began to part, revealing a waxing gibbous moon, by the time they made the two mile trek and reached the outskirt of land the house was on. They were both soaked, shivering, and covered in mud as they approached the old barn behind the house that looked like it could blow over if hit by a strong enough wind. Still, it seemed like the only spot for cover so they rushed over a twenty yard stretch of tall grass and pulled in close to the barn's old stone and mortar foundation. Many of the foundation stones had broken loose and were laying in the dirt. Vic stepped over them and followed behind Jones as they slowly crept around the barn and approached the corner where they were able to get a good view of the house which was dark with no exterior lighting on the property.

The wind blew strong and howled around them and the air was alive with buzzing night-time wildlife as they took a moment to catch their breath. Vic's senses were peaked, he slowed his breathing and felt a calm clarity set in that he had experienced before when in the middle of jobs like this. Jones put his bag on the ground, unzipped it, and started digging through. After a few moments, he pulled out an oddly shaped object which he put on his head and covered his eyes.

"Night-vision goggles," said Jones. "Sorry but I only got one."

Vic nodded in pleasant surprise. "No problem, what do you see?"

Jones moved his head back and forth as he scanned the area. "Looks clear, I'm not seeing anything around here."

Vic looked around as well, the gibbous moon provided faint illumination over the surrounding area. An apple tree was off to their right a few yards away that ran close to a wooden fence, and beyond that were vast stretches of recently plowed fields from a neighboring farm. Nothing looked out of place. Off to his left, the house still appeared as it had during their morning visit, looking ominous under the soft light of the moon.

"We're good," Jones stated. "Follow me."

They dashed towards the house as quietly as possible, approaching the boarded up rear basement window. Once there Jones nodded to Vic who opened his bag and pulled out a crowbar. He wedged the bar between the boarding and the foundation and gave a pull, the boarding came loose easily and Jones helped him remove it from the window. They set the boarding against the foundation and gave one last look around, not seeing any activity around the house.

"I'm going to go setup the cameras," said Jones. "Keep an eye out for me." He reached into his coat pocket and tossed something that Vic caught right before it was about to hit him in the head.

"It's a walkie-talkie. Press down on the button on the top right," Jones instructed.

Vic pressed it down and he heard a beep come from a second radio Jones had in his coat.

"No need to say anything, just press that button if you notice anything out of the ordinary. If you don't beep me first, I'll get you when I'm done."

Vic nodded and Jones turned around and lowered himself in through the window, leaving the night-vision goggles on. Vic watched him move further into the house then gave the surrounding area a scan. Everything still seemed clear. He crept towards the corner of the house by the apple tree and peered around the foundation. Far off in the distance, along the dirt road about a half mile away, a neighboring house showed signs of movement. The front porch lit up and moments later car headlights turned on. After a few seconds a car backed out and started heading down the road in the opposite direction. *Nothing to concern ourselves with,* Vic thought.

Sudden movement out of the corner of his eye drew his attention near the apple tree where a patch of grass met farmland, about thirty yards to his right. He stared intently at that area for a few seconds not seeing anything further, then decided to move towards it. Nearing the tree he noticed the ground was littered with apples that were never harvested. Abruptly, a small dark object darted away from behind the tree and into the field, Vic saw a white streak on top of it as it moved and knew immediately it was a skunk. He breathed a sigh of relief that it didn't spray, only to jerk in fear as he heard a noise behind and above him, a soft high-pitched wine which he realized was Jones drilling in the boarding on the second story window. He shook his head, he was getting spooked too easily.

The wind howled and picked up speed as high cirrus clouds passed overhead, occulting the moon. Shivering, he tucked his arms under his chest and glanced at the apples on the ground, wondering if they were any good. His stomach rumbled and his clothes were dirty, wet, and cold. Vic Abelson was not enjoying himself. There was nobody on this side of the house, of that he was certain, so he began moving back to check the other side. The barn stood to his left and the clouds parted again revealing the moon, which cast an eerie glow on the barn. A large chain secured the main doors in front. It seemed tilted slightly to the right, missing numerous wooden panels on its side, and its foundation was crumbling away. The thing looked like it could tip over from the wind at any second.

The other side of the house wasn't much different. More unkempt lawn near the house, more farmland beyond that. No trace of anybody nearby. He looked to the sky and saw flashes of light on the horizon, the storm Jones mentioned earlier appeared to be near. Vic crept back toward the house and sat down against the foundation, watching the storm in the distance. The wind picked up speed as it approached and the sound of distant thunder could be heard. He sat huddled there for a while before a noise from the back of the house drew his attention. He got up and peered around the corner to see Jones climbing out of the basement window. Vic met up with him.

"We're all set," whispered Jones. "Come on in."

Jones crept back down through the basement window. Vic followed and eased himself in, his feet hit the basement ground as he reached back out and pulled in his bag he had left by the window, placing it on the ground. He then reached out and moved the boarding back over the window, managing to get it in place. It wasn't very secure and if someone tried opening it he had no doubt it would easily fall open but at a casual glance from the outside it should look okay.

It was pitch black inside, Vic looked around not able to make anything out. He felt slightly uneasy. "Jones, where you at?" he whispered.

A light suddenly shone brightly in his face followed by a deep laughter as Jones stepped back and moved the flashlight out of Vic's eyes.

"Just seeing how easily you scare," said Jones with a smirk.

Vic leaned over and unzipped his bag, searching for a flashlight. He didn't want to get caught unaware by Jones again but decided to give a little back. "Careful. Sneak up on me like that again and I might accidentally shoot you."

Jones grunted, "Likewise."

Vic found the flashlight in his bag and flicked it on. A loud creaking noise caught his attention and he shone the light up toward the ceiling, seeing bare wooden trusses of the floor with some ventilation ducts and electrical wire housing running through.

"I was hearing all kinds of noises up there man," said Jones, looking up. "Wind seems to be playing this house like a chime. We should head up and check the cameras."

"Right behind you," replied Vic. He rubbed his arms and tried to get some warmth back in his body. While still cold, it was decidedly warmer inside without the wind biting through his wet clothes.

Jones threw a towel at him. "Clean yourself off as best you can. We don't want to leave a trial behind of every step we take."

Vic nodded and wiped off dirt and mud from his clothes and shoes as best he could, then left the dirty towel on the floor under the window. He grabbed his bag and followed Jones to the back corner of the basement then up a set of creaky wooden stairs to a landing on the first floor. At the top of the stairs, to his left, was an open door that led into a hallway that ran through the center of the house. A small bathroom was across the hall, to his right was the kitchen and dining room. Hardwood flooring creaked under his feet and the walls were covered with a vintage style wallpaper that was worn and peeling away. The air was thick as he breathed and had a musky odor which he assumed was mold. They turned left and Vic saw the front entry way with an open living room to the right and what looked like a smaller den or office to the left. Jones turned left and started heading up stairs that ran directly above the basement staircase.

Vic, recalling one of the news articles he read, turned right into the living room. *Marcus' body was found on the first floor living room*, the article had read. *He was shot four times with one of the gunshot wounds having occurred prior to his arrival at the house.*

Vic panned his flashlight back and forth across the hardwood flooring and noticed a large dark circle in the hardwood along the outer wall, under a window. He bent over, took off his glove, and brushed his hand over the area. It felt cold, cooler than the rest of the house felt. That seemed odd to Vic.

"You coming up man?" Jones shouted from the top of the stairs. "I could have sworn you were right behind me."

"Yeah, I'm coming," he called back. Vic put his glove back on and headed toward the stairs.

"I setup shop in the master bedroom," Jones said as Vic grabbed onto the railing and began climbing. "Only the second floor has windows in every direction. Plus, it leaves the first floor clear in case someone comes snooping unexpectedly."

"Let's hope nobody decides to come snooping," replied Vic as he climbed the stairs. It seemed that every step creaked as he put his weight on it, and a couple of the boards wobbled. As he neared the top, the wooden railing he held with his left hand continued up and bent back around to run parallel with the stairs on the second floor hallway. It had a couple posts missing. There were doors at both ends of the hallway and two in the middle as well. Vic saw wires running along the floor from each doorway, except from the first one on his left which appeared to be the bathroom, leading to a room in front of him where Jones stood. All the cables led to a small laptop resting on the floor of this room. There were four images in each corner of the screen. Vic looked onscreen and didn't see anything that caught his attention.

"We're still good," Jones confirmed. "Seems quiet outside. What were you doing down there?"

"Looking for the spot where Marcus died. I was thinking of maybe starting there and trying to backtrack his movements," replied Vic. "See if we can figure out where he was and what he was doing while he was here."

Jones nodded, "Not a bad idea, maybe he left some clues behind as to where he hid them. Did you find it?"

"I think so, there's a stain on the hardwood underneath the living room window that looks like it may have been blood. Guess I was hoping to just see the white outline of a body. Do police even do that anymore?"

"Not that I'm aware of," replied Jones, shaking his head. "Once they close out the investigation they clean the place up as best they can. As I understand it forensics did their work here over the course of two weeks then split."

Vic was suddenly concerned. "Do you think the authorities could have found the diamonds?"

Jones shook his head. "No, they just had two dead bodies on their hands and were trying to figure out what led them to die here. While I'm sure they checked out the house, they weren't aware of these diamonds and wouldn't have known to search for them. Nothing I've read indicates they found any notable items when they did their investigation."

"Yeah, I guess we better start looking," said Vic, glancing around. "Any thoughts on what to look for? Are the diamonds in a pouch of some sort or you think they're loose somewhere?"

"You're guess is as good as mine," replied Jones. He looked up as a gust of wind made the ceiling creak.

Vic frowned while looking up as well. "You mentioned they were cursed and I never asked. What kind of curse are we dealing with here? That's kind of vague."

Jones shrugged again looking back to Vic, "Don't tell me you believe in that sort of thing. Dean just said they had a dark history, were *really* valuable, and are cursed. I focused on *valuable*, and left it at that."

Vic nodded, unsure if he should press Jones any further on the subject. "Well, I'm going to go back downstairs and see if I can find any way to retrace Marcus' steps."

The wind blew strong outside and shook the rafters in the ceiling again, causing both of them to look up. "Told you man," Jones began, "we're going to be hearing stuff like that all damn night. Don't let it get to you." Jones looked around the master bedroom, thoughtful. "You check out downstairs, I wanna check this room out. I had a weird feeling when setting things up here and just want to look around a little more. Oh, and one more thing," Jones nodded toward the flashlight Vic held. "Try not to use that flashlight all the time, just when you really need to see. Not sure if any light can leak out from the holes I drilled or around the boards." Jones reached into his bag by the laptop and pulled out a flashlight that he threw to Vic. "Use this one anytime you're by the windows. It's what pilots use on night flights, helps them see better and keeps their eyes adjusted to the dark."

Vic turned his regular flashlight off, then the one Jones gave him on and was surprised by the gentle red illuminance it shone. "How am I supposed to find red diamonds with a red flashlight?"

"I was told you were someone who got things done," Jones quipped. "I'm sure you'll figure it out."

Vic smirked and turned around, panning the flashlight back and forth along the hallway. It cast an eerie red glow but he was able to see pretty well with it once his eyes started adjusting.

"Shit!" exclaimed Jones.

"What is it?" asked Vic, turning back around. Jones was watching the laptop. In the camera image on the upper right corner of the screen he saw headlights coming down the road toward the house. Vic watched as a car slowed as it approached, coming out of the camera's view in the upper right and moving into the upper left camera's view of the front of the house facing the road. As it moved closer to the center of view a beeping noise came from the laptop and a curser hovered over the area with movement on screen. At least the motion sensing software worked, Vic noted.

"Fuck, we're just getting started," said Vic. He looked to Jones. "What's the plan?"

"You keep watching, I'm going to head down to the basement," Jones said calmly.

"What are you going to do?"

"If anyone gets out and starts snooping around the house, hit the button on the walkie-talkie. If anyone comes in through the basement, I'll deal with it." Jones pulled out a silenced pistol and headed out the door and down the stairs.

Vic turned his attention back to the screen, trying his best to suppress the fear that coursed through him.

CHAPTER 4

Unwelcome

J ones rushed downstairs while Vic sat down in the bedroom, intently watching the screen. The car was stopped on the opposite side of the road in front of the house with its headlights on. Vic checked the time on his watch, noting it was 9:03 p.m. About a minute passed with no activity when the headlights turned off and the driver's door opened. Someone stepped out but he could only make out a dark silhouette on-screen.

"Shit," Vic uttered under his breath. The person started approaching the house. He hit the button on the top right of his walkie-talkie.

As the person approached the house Vic noticed they seemed to move with the gait of a man wearing a dark trench coat, and who slowed as he approached the house, eyeing the area to his left. Something must have caught his attention. *Hopefully the skunk was still around that apple tree,* Vic thought.

The man stopped in his tracks and reached inside his coat, appearing to answer a cellphone. He then turned around and walked quickly back to his car and got in. Headlights came on and the car lurched forward and drove away from the house. Vic watched it move down the road and let out a sigh of relief when it was no longer in view.

"We're all clear, you can head back up," Vic called over the radio. He waited as he heard the creak of floorboards and stairs as Jones made his way back up to the bedroom.

"What happened?" asked Jones as he walked in, short of breath.

"It appeared to be a man who got out of the car and started approaching the house so I hit the button to signal you," Vic began, "but it looks like he got a phone call and got back in his car and drove away."

Jones nodded, looking concerned. "I wonder who that was." He looked to Vic. "We gotta do this quickly. That person might decide to come back, or some other unwelcome visitor."

Vic agreed and got up off the floor, he couldn't help but feel like they were the unwelcome visitors tonight. Something about this house made him feel very uneasy, and it wasn't just the fact that they were in the middle of a break-in, he had gotten used to *that* feeling. It was something he couldn't put his finger on. "What were you going to check out in here? Not much to search through." Vic glanced around the barren master bedroom. Aside from the laptop on the floor there wasn't really anything else that caught his attention. The closet doors were missing and the closet itself was empty though he noticed a hatch in the ceiling to access the attic.

"Like I said, I got a weird feeling when I was setting up in this room," replied Jones. "Maybe there's a loose board or something somewhere. I just figured I'd start here. Plus after what just happened it wouldn't hurt to have someone close to the laptop."

Vic nodded, "Alright. I'm going to have a look around this floor real quick then head back down to try and retrace Marcus's steps."

Jones just grunted and looked around the bedroom, appearing thoughtful. Vic pulled out his regular flashlight and flicked it on as he walked into the hallway. He turned into the first door on his right which was a bathroom and the mirror above the sink reflected back the bright light of the flashlight and had a layer of film over it which distorted his reflection. The mirror had a handle which he pulled open to reveal an empty medicine cabinet. Below the sink was another cabinet he went through looking for any crevices that could be used to hide the diamonds, not finding any. He glanced at the toilet.

"Son of a bitch," Vic muttered. He lifted the lid to the toilet and was disturbed to find the bowl had a disgusting layer of filth that looked a little too close to shit for his comfort. The house had been winterized for some time now so there was no water at the bottom but still, a thought occurred to him and he had to check. Resigned to do what he had to do he pulled off his glove and brought his hand down and felt around in bottom of the bowl, bringing his hand in as far as he could reach. It was cold and slimy but he felt nothing inside. Disgusted, he brought his hand back and stared at it, regretting the fact that he didn't have a cloth or paper towel readily available. Sensing a presence behind him, he turned around to see Jones staring at him, eyes bewildered.

"Find anything?"

"I'd say I didn't find shit," replied Vic, "but that may not be entirely true."

Jones grunted and threw a small piece of cloth at him. "You need to be a little more prepared before sticking your hand in places it's not meant to be." Jones nodded toward the cloth. "You keep that, I got a couple more. Plus I got a box of latex gloves. All you need to do is ask man."

"Yeah, that would have been nice to know." Vic wiped off his hand as best he could and stuffed the cloth in one of his coat pockets, figuring he might need it later. He got up and turned around to head out but held up for a second. He turned back around and grabbed the porcelain lid covering the reservoir tank and looked inside. It was empty, other than a little mold scattered throughout. The rubber stopper that the handle connected to covered a little hole at the bottom that he reached in and opened, shining the flashlight in. It looked empty but he stuck his fingers in as far as he could and felt nothing. He put the lid back on. There wasn't anything else to search in there.

"I don't think they're in here," he said to Jones.

"Well, I like your thoroughness," Jones replied, watching him with amusement.

"I think it would only be fair if you checked the downstairs bathroom."

"We'll cross that bridge when we get there." Jones replied then headed back into the master bedroom.

Vic inspected the shower which had a layer of dust and filth on it as well and concluded that no one had used or tried to hide anything in that drain in years due to the undisturbed layer on grime over it. He walked out of the bathroom and over to the master bedroom and grabbed a pair of latex gloves from Jones and put them in his pocket. He then cleaned his hands with some sanitizer he brought and put his regular gloves back on to keep his hands warm. Jones inspected the closet area and Vic walked back out of the room.

He was about to check out the bloodstain downstairs when something caught his attention in the room down the hall on the right. He could of swore he saw a little green ball of light in the doorway and walked down the hall to investigate. He pulled out the red flashlight Jones had given him and flicked it on. Vic was impressed Jones knew these were the flashlights used by pilots on night flights, using them here made sense the more he thought about it but the flashlight cast an eerie red glow around the small room and the dream Vic had earlier popped in his mind. The fear of having been caught returned but he did his best to control what he was feeling.

It wasn't difficult searching the smallest of the three bedrooms. There was no furniture or any objects in the room to inspect. An open vent caught his attention so he put on one of the latest gloves and reached in and stuck his hand down as far as it could go but didn't feel anything suspicious. Opening the closet he saw a shelf that ran along the upper wall with a bar for hanging clothes. He had to jump to check the shelf but it was empty and dusty on top. There didn't seem to be anything that could have caused the green light he saw.

As he was about to turn around and leave, he noticed something odd that caught his eye. It was barely noticeable at first, and hard to make out due to the red light, but after kneeling down he made out a strange stain on the lower portion of the wall above the floor trim. It looked similar to the stain he saw downstairs.

"Jones," Vic called out while grabbing his other flashlight, "come check this out."

Jones quickly rushed into the room, intrigued. "What do you got?"

"It looks to me like a blood stain on the wall from a hand that smeared it on," said Vic. He turned the normal flashlight on so he could see the stain more clearly.

"Yeah man, I see it. Looks like a bloody hand smeared against there," said Jones, looking around. "It's on the trim and floor too."

Vic had noticed that now as well. He reached down and tried to pull on the trim. It was stuck securely to the wall. He tried moving the hardwood flooring pieces but everything seemed locked in place. "I don't know, nothings budging. That had to have been from Marcus, I wonder what he was doing up here."

"You know," Jones began, eyebrows creased in thought, "I thought I saw something similar in the master bedroom but I thought it was just a normal stain. We should check that out."

Vic nodded and they got up and walked back to the master bedroom, sparing a glance at the laptop screen to make sure nobody was outside. Jones walked to the corner of the room and shined his light on the wall around the floorboards. Vic put his regular glove back on as he moved.

"See, there's another one," said Jones, crouching on his

hands and knees by the discoloration in the wood. "Dried up blood on the trim and floorboards." Jones tried to move the trim then checked the flooring for any loose boards. Everything seemed tight.

"Maybe he intentionally left those to throw off whoever was looking for them," Vic offered. "I'm thinking we might find stains like this all over the house."

Jones appeared thoughtful, "Could be."

Suddenly, the flashlight Jones was holding went out followed by a somewhat loud knocking noise behind them, making Vic's heart skip a beat.

"What the hell was that?" Vic heard Jones curse while quickly turning around. The screen of the laptop illuminated the room, revealing nothing that could have caused the noise. Jones walked over to where the noise came from, in the corner of the room. "Shine your light over here."

Vic did as instructed, pointing his flashlight where Jones signaled. "I think I see a blood stain there too."

Jones reached over, feeling around the stained area. Vic noticed something then that sent shivers down his body. "Jones, look at your breath."

Jones stared down as he exhaled, his breath was misting heavily. "Holy shit," he said, sounding slightly frantic. "It wasn't doing that before." He reached out his hand, moving it back and forth through the air over the blood stain. "It seems really cold here. I feel all tingly, excited. I'm not normally like this."

Vic started to feel unsettled, he had been feeling the same just then and thought back to the night he spent with Shelly watching that show. He *had* thought it was a bunch of crap at the time, after all he had come to not fear the dark as a kid, but now he was trying to rationalize what just happened and was having a hard time coming to a logical conclusion.

"Alright," Vic began uncertainly, "this house has been making some weird noises all night, it's windy out and this place is old and unsteady. There's probably just a draft coming from somewhere and that noise was probably just caused by the wind against the house. I think we're making a little too much of this right now."

"Yeah, maybe," replied Jones, uncertain. "But I just put brand new batteries in all these flashlights when I was prepping for tonight. My flashlight shouldn't have died just now."

"Maybe the light just went out. Electronics break on occasion, bulbs burn out." Vic offered.

"Yeah, I suppose," he said, looking at the dead flashlight in his hand. He didn't appear to fully agree with that explanation.

To be honest, Vic didn't really believe in what he was saying either. During the show he watched, the group also experienced similar occurrences like cold spots and feeling a static charge in the air. He recalled they attributed it to paranormal energy.

Jones got up, eying the laptop, "I need to take a piss. I'm going outside for minute."

Vic needed to go as well and the thought of staying in the house alone was a little disconcerting at the moment. "Think I'll join you."

Vic followed Jones as they made their way down both staircases and into the basement. The boarding on the window came off easily and they slipped outside. Low dark clouds continued to slowly pass overhead and flashes of lightning lit up the sky with thunder rolling not too far away. It looked like it was about to start pouring any minute now. Jones walked to one of corner of the house and Vic took the other corner. The air felt cool and refreshing to Vic as it was easier breathe than the thick moldy air that filled the house, and a fog in his head seemed to clear. Vic finished up and met up with Jones who was waiting for him by the window. Lightning flashed, quickly followed by thunder and Vic heard the first drops of rain start to fall.

"Let's take a look at that spot where Marcus died, see how it compares to the other stains we saw," said Vic.

"Alright, after you," replied Jones, gesturing his hand towards the basement window. Vic climbed in and Jones followed. Vic reached back out and moved the boarding back in place then they proceeded upstairs to the first floor where Vic led Jones to the living room. He knelt down near the blood stain on the floor, it was easily discernible even with the red flashlight he used since they were close to a window.

"I read in one of the news articles that Marcus was waiting in ambush for the men that rushed in the house looking for him. He shot one as they entered," Vic gestured toward the boarded up front door, "killing one, and then getting shot in return. He died right here." Jones was watching him intently as he spoke though he remained silent. "When you were heading upstairs that first time we came in I saw this spot and when I reached with my hand it felt really cold here, like out of place cold, as it was upstairs earlier."

Jones rolled his eyes and took a deep breath. "So what exactly are you trying to say?"

Vic didn't know what he believed right now. He never experienced anything like this before in his life. "I'm not sure anymore man, but this is too coincidental to..." his voice trailed off. Jones' eyes widened. He heard it too.

They both looked up.

Right above their heads, moving ever so slowly, was the soft creaking of footsteps coming from the room above them. They each remained frozen as the steps slowly led to what Vic assumed was out of the spare bedroom he had just searched earlier, then into the hallway, to where they stopped right at the top of the stairs.

"There's nobody upstairs," whispered Jones in disbelief. "There can't be anybody upstairs, we just searched those rooms."

Vic slowly rose, trying his best to keep his hand steady. He pointed his flashlight towards the staircase, illuminating it in red. Jones quickly shone his light there as well, filling it with a more natural light. The stairs ran up past the ceiling, not revealing anything unusual. Jones pulled out his pistol. Vic did the same with his free hand.

"Turn that thing off," Jones uttered. Vic obliged him, turning off the red light.

They slowly crept towards the stairs, senses peaked and guns drawn. Vic was certain he could hear a pin drop if one fell. As they moved, more and more of the upper staircase revealed itself until the flashlight cleared the ceiling, revealing the top of the staircase. Jones stood next to him. Both had guns pointed to where the flashlight shone.

Nobody was there.

Vic felt a sudden icy coolness surround him. He looked over and saw mist coming from Jones' mouth as he breathed. A sharp rush of air hit him in the back of the neck while he heard what sounded like a person exhaling loudly between them. Vic and Jones jumped at the same time.

"Tell me that was you," Jones yelled, dropping his gun to his side. He had a stone-cold seriousness to him. "Tell me that was you who just took that fucking breath!" Jones shone the flashlight in his face.

Vic stared back, speechless. He put his hands up, shaking his head.

"Holy shit, holy shit," Jones kept repeating for a couple seconds, turning around and around frantically.

"Alright, we need to calm down," Vic said, firmly. "Keep it together." He was having a damn hard time of it himself, his whole body was tense. This was against everything he'd grown up believing.

Jones crouched down, burying his face in his hands. "Okay, okay," he said taking a deep breath. He started rubbing his temples. "We can deal with this. We have to deal with this."

Vic looked around, uncertain. He listened for any odd noise and looked for anything unnatural but didn't notice anything else. It seemed like whatever caused the things they just experienced had left for now. "I'm not feeling it anymore."

"Me neither," said Jones, looking around meekly.

"We should head back upstairs and regroup," said Vic, looking up the staircase. "We need a plan of attack here and we'll need to be ready to just stand our ground if anything like that happens again." A certain resolve started filling Vic, overcoming the fear he'd been experiencing. Those guys on television made their way through a much scarier place than this, he and Jones could do the same.

Something in Vic's voice must have moved Jones as well as he saw Jones stand up and look like he was getting a grip on himself. "Okay, let's do this. You first." Jones nodded towards the stairs.

Vic let out a quick breath, which was the best laugh he could muster at the moment. Vic shone his flashlight up the stairs and began walking up. The first step wobbled, startling Vic for a second, but he continued on. They slowly made their way up, about halfway a loud thunderclap shook the house, scaring Vic and Jones. Rain started to beat down heavily. After pausing for a moment, Vic continued on and once he reached the top quickly noticed that the laptop in the bedroom had gone blank. It looked like it either shut down or had run out of power and it only added to the tension he was feeling right now. They didn't have any eyes on the outside.

"What happened to your laptop?" asked Vic. "Would it just power down like that?"

"No man, it's setup to just keep running," replied Jones, sounding frustrated. "This isn't good, we're in the dark here." Jones knelt down and started checking connections on the laptop, also checking that the battery was secure. He slid over to his bag and started going through it. "Give me some light over here."

Vic walked over and shone his light in Jones' bag, noticing he had a good amount of supplies in there: a crowbar, mallet, power tools, flashlights, extra batteries, and that was only a portion of what Vic was able to see. Thunder continued to roll and strong gusts of wind shook the rafters along with waves of rain that pounded against the side of the house—all only adding to Vic's unease. The good news was at least no one would be out in this kind of weather snooping around outside.

"Got it," Jones stated, holding up a slim object. He went back to the laptop and flipped it over, pulling out the battery and replaced it with the one he just pulled from the bag, double checking that it was secure. He flipped the laptop back over and set it on the ground then pushed the power button. The screen on the laptop lit up for a second then went blank again and remained still.

"What the hell is going on?" Jones asked, inspecting the laptop more closely. Vic could tell he was starting to get angry.

"How long is that battery supposed to last?" asked Vic.

"Each battery is supposed to last four to six hours," replied Jones, scratching his head. "I fully charged both of them before I left."

"What are we going to do?" asked Vic. He knew this had to be attributed to the paranormal activity they witnessed earlier. Shelly had mentioned that she had seen episodes where spirits use energy from electronic devices or even people to help manifest activity. Vic didn't feel like that was something he needed to mention to Jones right now, he appeared to be having a hard time coming to grips with what was going on and this left them in a vulnerable position. They needed to be able to see what was going on outside the house.

Jones held his face in his palms, letting out a sigh. "We need to abort for the night. We can't go on without these cameras working."

Vic started to object, but he couldn't find any good reason that would allow them to continue.

"We still got time, there's no immediate need to get this done tonight," said Jones. "The diamonds will still be waiting for us tomorrow. I need to go back and see what's going on with this laptop."

Vic couldn't argue. He nodded to Jones, accepting defeat for the night. "Alright we'll head back. I think we have a good feel for this place though. We'll need to work up a more thorough way to search as I just think we could attack this a little differently than we did tonight."

58

Jones looked and nodded in agreement. "Yeah, we're sort of wandering in the dark about how to find these. We'll work on our plan. For the moment, I need to get the cameras and everything in order. Why don't you grab your stuff and be on the lookout outside for me?"

"Yeah, no problem." Vic grabbed his bag and headed out and down the stairs. The steps creaked and the house moaned with the strong wind and pounding rain but Vic didn't notice anything out of the ordinary as he made his way down through the basement to the window. Vic saw the rain was really coming down and figured no one would be foolish enough to be snooping around on a night like this, but he got out and scouted around the house. As expected, he didn't see any signs of anybody in the area so he crawled back in the basement and waited by the window.

In the small amount of time he was out there he had gotten sopping wet. He was considering going back up to tell Jones that they should stay a little longer due to the heavy rain but it began to ease up as he was considering it. He recalled Jones said the thunderstorm would pass by and it would clear up soon after. Besides, he was dripping wet and cold, and wanted to leave anyway. No sense taking any further risks.

The rain had slowed to a trickle by the time Jones walked down the steps into the basement. He walked up beside Vic and peeked his head out the window then turned back to him. "Is this your idea of keeping a look out?"

Vic shrugged, trying to act nonchalant. "I went out and had a look around. It let up a bit but I don't think anyone would be crazy enough to be outside when it was pouring a few minutes ago."

Jones looked like he was about to say something but then appeared to notice that fact that Vic was pretty soaked and shaking and just looked back out the window. "We'll give it few more minutes then head out. Maybe some of this equipment got wet on the way here and that's what's causing this shit. No point in getting it wet again if we don't have too."

Vic nodded in agreement. They waited in silence, each looking gloomily out the window. The house continued to creak and Vic thought he heard some weird noises coming from upstairs but did his best to ignore them, figuring his mind was manipulating normal sounds. Within a few minutes the rain ceased and Jones picked up his bag and shoved it out the window. Then he pulled himself up and out. Vic did the same then secured the boarding in place. They each surveyed the area and gave it the all clear.

"Let's go," said Jones.

They dashed across the lawn to the barn and held close to its foundation as they made their way around the perimeter to the creek that would lead them on the two mile journey back to the car. The wind still blew strong and the clouds in the sky partially cleared revealing the waxing gibbous moon which had risen higher in the sky. Flashes still lit up the horizon in the direction the storm was traveling. Hopefully the weather won't be a factor next time.

Once they reached the creek and began following it, Vic frequently looked up to the moon as his mind raced with the events that just transpired. It seemed like things he had been raised to believe were turning around on him. For a second in that house he thought he might lose his cool. It seemed that it nearly got the better of Jones who trudged along the creek in silence with his head down, seeming morose. Vic started to feel like he had earlier, that him and Jones were just unwelcome visitors in the house and that whatever was with them earlier was asserting that the house was theirs and that they needed to leave. Vic pondered this the rest of way back.

When they reached the car, it was exactly as they left it. Jones groaned as he opened the trunk and hefted his bag in. Vic felt relief too as he placed his in, getting that weight off his shoulders felt incredible. He looked down at his clothes—he was wet, muddy, cold, and weary to the bone. While they didn't have the diamonds he was looking forward to getting back to the motel and taking a hot shower, which he almost wanted more at that moment.

Jones threw a blanked at Vic. "Take off your coat and pants, your filthy."

Vic grabbed it and did as he was told then wrapped himself with the blanket. The wet clothes he wore clung to his skin but he was glad to finally get some of them off. He placed them in the trunk and got in the car.

Jones placed a towel on the driver's seat and got in. He started up the Caddy then slowly pulled out of the hiding spot, leaving the lights off until they were sure it was clear then proceeded onto the road. Vic glanced at the clock in the dash, it was almost midnight. The first night in and they only managed to make it maybe three hours in the house. That wasn't good. Vic looked to Jones who was focused on the road and didn't look like he wanted to talk so Vic rode under the moonlit night in silence.

Vic stopped shivering and was starting to feel warm when they pulled back in the motel. Jones dropped him off in front of his room and popped the trunk.

"Stop by when you're up and about tomorrow," Jones said as Vic got out of car. He nodded then walked around and grabbed his clothes and bag then closed the trunk, giving it a bump to let Jones know he was good.

Once inside his room, Vic stripped off the rest of his clothes and headed directly to the shower. He turned the water up close to burning and let the filth of the day wash off. After he was clean he stayed in the shower for a while, letting the warm water wash over and ease his achy muscles. He would have stayed in longer but after a few minutes the water started cooling off so he got out and dried himself with a towel.

Vic spent the rest of the night reflecting on the events that took place in the house, planning on how to get the diamonds. Well into the night, he drifted off to sleep, leaving the light on.

CHAPTER 5

The Buyer

Vic sat in the corner of a small, brightly-lit room with white padded walls, his backside pressed against padding behind him and the rest of his body pressed against the adjoining wall. A white straitjacket held his arms across his torso and he wore loose white trousers with bare feet. The whiteness of the walls gave the illusion the room was bigger than it actually was, yet at the same time he felt horribly confined and trapped.

Time passed. No clock hung on the wall so Vic was unable to judge how long he sat there, all the while wondering why he was there to begin with. It was cold and no blanket was in sight so he pressed close against the wall, temple resting against the soft padding that offered little warmth. Everything was still and quiet.

Suddenly the lights shut off and the room went pitch black. Vic felt a presence nearby. Nothing stirred and no sounds were heard but he couldn't shake the feeling that someone, or something, was watching him.

The lights turned back and on and he saw Shelly in the opposite corner of the room. She also wore the same white straitjacket with white trousers and was hunched in the corner, but she had a horrified expression on her face and held her hands up in a defensive posture, appearing to struggle with something Vic couldn't see. He went to go help her but his limbs wouldn't respond, he was paralyzed and unable to move.

The lights went out again. Vic looked in Shelly's direction and gasped, seeing two small red orbs glowing in the opposite corner of the room, staring back at him. They didn't belong to Shelly, they were something else—their own entity. He could feel the eyes piercing into him, cutting through the flesh and exposing his weaknesses and fear.

"Look," he heard a voice whisper from no direction in particular as the lights came back on and eyes disappeared. He was alone in the room again, Shelly was nowhere to be seen. Vic looked down as the creases separating the square padding on the floor grew dark red and a thick fluid started to rise through the cracks. He watched in alarm as the white padding on the floor became covered in red, climbing the perimeter of each pad until the highest point in the center where it could no longer resist the rising tide. Vic realized it was blood seeping up through the cracks in the ground. He could feel it, thick on his feet and soaking into his trousers, warm and sticky. He tried to move yet remained paralyzed, his fear intensified.

In the opposite corner of the room where Shelly had been, the head of a serpent rose from the crimson surface, its eyes fixated on Vic's. It stared at him for a while then slithered forward, slow and mesmeric, through the shallow pool of blood in the room. It paused in the middle of the room, nonchalantly, seeming to know its prey was already caught and snared. A forked tongue emerged as it gave a gentle hiss. It appeared almost curious in him.

Vic could only watch the creature in fear as he willed and struggled to move his body, all to no avail. The serpent drew closer until it was right in front of him, it had to be at least six feet long. It's forked tongue flicked as it gave another hiss, it appeared to be taking in Vic's scent, when without warning it snapped forward and sunk its fangs into Vic's thigh. Vic jolted forward in shock and pain only to find that he was sitting up in his motel room bed. He stared blankly ahead for a while, taking deep breaths and letting his heartbeat recede.

Bad dreams were nothing new to Vic, he had good and bad dreams all his life but this one felt different somehow. It was more vivid and felt hauntingly real. The terror he felt still coursed through him and he looked down to his leg where the serpent bit, there was no wound, mark, or pain. Once his heartbeat felt back to normal he turned to the alarm clock on the side of the bed, it was 11:13 a.m.

With a long sigh, he stretched and swung his legs over the side of the bed, letting his feet hit the floor. His head hurt. He sat on the side of the bed hunched over for a while, rubbing his temples with his palms then cradling his head in his hands. After a couple minutes he grabbed his cell phone from the nightstand and entered a number. It took three rings before a familiar voice answered.

"Hey you," said Shelly, endearingly. "How's my man doing?"

"I'm doing fine. How are you? I miss you."

"I'm doing alright. I miss you too," replied Shelly. "I've been thinking of you. Is everything okay?"

Vic spoke reassuringly, "Yeah, things are fine. I'm still in DeKalb outside of Chicago, we finished loading the truck and are going to be heading out soon. I'm free at the moment, so thought I'd check in." Truth be told, he just needed to hear her voice again. It soothed and helped clear his head of the dream and events of the night before.

"Oh, you didn't have to do that," she replied, "but since you asked, my sister was over yesterday. She's been having trouble with her boyfriend again..."

Vic spent the next half hour listening to her talk about her sister, and then about work and other things. He would chime in when asked or to offer his opinion. After a time the visions from the dreams faded and he began to feel normal. A beeping on the line started coming through, someone was calling. He told Shelly to hold on for a second.

"Yeah?" he asked after switching lines.

"Vic, head over to my room," said Jones. "We need to talk."

"Give me a couple minutes," replied Vic.

"Alright."

Vic looked down and switched the line back to Shelly. "Hey baby, sorry but I need to get back to work. I'll talk with you later."

"Okay, thanks for calling. Bye sweetie," she replied warmly.

"Bye babe," he replied tenderly.

It was a little after noon by the time Vic had washed up, changed clothes, and headed out the door. He walked down to room 113 then gave a hard knock. Jones quickly opened and gestured for him to come in, closing the door behind him.

Vic scanned the room, seeing not much had changed from the last time he was here. Clothes were still scattered haphazardly around the room. Trash lay strewn about. Vic was almost certain the pizza box he saw on the floor was the same one from the other day. The duffel bag with all his work equipment lay in the corner seemingly untouched from the night before.

Jones himself had seen better days. He looked like he hadn't showered since they got back. Dark circles hung under his eyes and Vic wrinkled his nose at the foul odor that seemed to be coming from Jones' direction.

"You sleep well?" Jones asked gruffly, eyes locked on Vic's.

White padded walls with a serpent biting into his leg filled his mind but he didn't think now would be a good time to mention that. "Yeah, I slept well enough."

Jones rushed him, shoving him into the wall behind him with his right hand. Unrelenting, his grip held on to Vic's left shoulder just above the collar bone, pinning him against the wall.

"Don't fucking lie to me," said Jones, angrily. "Do you think I'd have made it where I'm at in life without being able to tell when I'm being lied to? *Did* you sleep well? Did your fluffy pillows and clean sheets take you off to a nice cozy slumberland where sheep jump over wooden fences spanning green pastures and rainbows dance in the sky?" His voice had taken on a mocking tone toward the end.

Shocked, Vic didn't know what to make of this but felt angry. "No!" he yelled, pushing Jones back. He pictured he was in the white room again, serpent uncoiling, Shelly struggling with an unknown foe. "Fine, you want the truth? The truth is I didn't sleep well! I had some fucked up dreams full of blood and horror, and I couldn't do anything about it. I couldn't even move!" Vic's hands were clenched.

That seemed to satisfy Jones, he stepped back and nodded toward the bed. "Good, have a seat."

Vic stared back at Jones for second, then shook his head and moved toward the bed, throwing a pair of pants that were strewn across the bed on the floor before he sat down.

"Now," Jones began somewhat coolly, starting to act more like himself, "there's something I didn't tell you about the diamonds. Dean mentioned it to me in passing before I took the job, said his buyer thought he'd mention it as it might be of some importance. Now I didn't buy into it at the time as normally I don't believe in that type of shit, but after what's been happening lately, I think you need to know. It was on my mind all night after things started getting weird."

Vic started feeling unsettled. "Okay, I'm listening." He shifted around in the bed, suddenly unable to get comfortable.

"I got the feeling Dean didn't exactly share with me all the details he might have known about this, but he did say that his buyer had been trying to get his hands on these diamonds for quite some time now. Not only because of their monetary worth, that goes without question, but he seems to feel that these diamonds can hold some sort of power over people. They can influence a persons behavior, manipulate the environment around them, even slip into someone's dreams."

"You did say they were cursed but," Vic paused, trying to organize his thoughts. The dreams he had been having lately were more vivid than dreams typically were for him. Could what he had been experiencing in them be influenced by the diamonds, or just random messages from his subconscious?

"I told you man, I didn't believe it myself. I thought it was the notion of some stupid ass rich dude who read too many books," said Jones, perplexed. "But now I'm having some fucked up dreams—and the shit that happened last night. I just don't know any more man."

Vic didn't know what to say. He was dealing with the same doubt. The dreams and the unexplained phenomena last night were unlike anything he experienced before.

"I talked to Dean after dropping you off yesterday," said Jones. "He's gonna hit us up, along with the buyer, to offer up some suggestions on how to continue. They should be calling anytime now."

Vic nodded and took a deep breath. He felt exhausted and had a feeling the sleep he had gotten wasn't exactly the restful type. He leaned back and was disgusted to realize he was laying in more of Jones' dirty laundry.

"Here," Jones offered, clearing items off the recliner in the room, "have a seat. I need to clean up here anyway."

Jones went about cleaning up the room, piling trash in the garbage container and then around it when it became full. Vic sat in the chair watching Jones. His head was swirling with thoughts of the job, the diamonds, and Shelly. Twenty minutes had passed when Jones' cell phone rang and Jones ran to pick it up off the table.

"Hello?" Jones answered, placing the phone by his ear. "Dean, thanks for calling. Yeah, he's here. Let me put this on speaker." Jones pressed down on the screen of his smartphone and placed it on the table between him and Vic.

"Vic, how are you holding up?" asked Dean, his elderly

voice sounded genuinely concerned.

"I'm hanging in there. I know we'd appreciate any assistance you can give us on this," he said.

"Of course, you know I'm here for you guys. I don't normally do this, but I reached out to our buyer and he's willing to offer some assistance with our predicament. For the purposes of this conversation, you can refer to him as Al. I got Al on the line, let me link him in." Dean went silent for a second and Vic heard a buzz over the smartphone speaker.

"Al, what can you offer up to our friends here?" asked Dean.

"Gentleman," a voice came through with a very distinct Middle-Eastern accent. "I heard that your search has turned up some unusual results. First, let me say that while it may not seem so, what you have been experiencing lately is, in my opinion, a sign of great hope. I say that as I believe this means you are close to finding what we seek. Very close indeed! Please do not lose faith now. From what I heard you have been experiencing some trouble sleeping among other things. Is that correct?"

"Yeah, you can say that," replied Jones.

"Well, that is to be expected," stated Al, he spoke with meticulous pronunciation. "I'd like to tell you about the Red Diamond Eyes. Not many know their history like I do."

"Yes, please," said Vic. "We'd like as much information as we can get."

"Excellent. Now the Red Diamond Eyes are not very old to be honest, as far as cut diamonds go. They originated from the Argyle Diamond Mine located in a remote area in Northwestern Australia. As it happens, that mine is one of the primary sources of diamonds in the world. The majority of diamonds produced there are brown diamonds, which are not gem quality, and they turn out a good percentage of yellow, white, even pink and blue gem quality diamonds. However, on occasion, that mine is known to be one of the only sources in the world where the conditions allow for genuine red diamonds. The coloring is a defect actually, an impurity of nitrogen in the crystal lattice that causes the diamond to change its hue."

Vic wasn't sure this information was especially useful for their search, but he allowed Al to continue.

"Most of the coloring detracts from the diamond's value as it results in a dull brown or yellow tint, even though some clever salesmen have gotten around to calling the brown ones *chocolate* diamonds to entice the buyer, but when levels are correct—to the minutest detail—it allows certain hues to shine. So it was on a blistering summer day one-hundred and eighty years ago, a handful of miners stumbled upon one of the most impressive of finds, in the deepest, purest red they had ever seen. Knowing its value at first glance, the small group of miners banded together and sought to keep it for themselves and sell it on their own. Unfortunately for them, the owners of the mine had been running the operation for a long time and had checks in place to keep such events from happening. It was here, before the diamonds were even cut, that the envy for these beautiful stones led to the first shedding of blood."

Vic leaned closer to the speaker, wanting to make sure he picked up everything that Al was saying.

"One of the miners who witnessed the discovery, who was an outsider to the group, felt worried that he was going to be cheated out of his share of the sale and reported the find, along with the conspiracy to hide it, to the mine owners who quickly took the find and punished the conspirators. No official report came out detailing what happened to the miners, however, they were never seen again. The outsider who reported them was paid handsomely and many years later was the one to tell the story."

Al paused for a moment and spoke off the phone in a language Vic couldn't understand but was back without missing a beat. "Now, once the rare stone was in the hands of the mine owners they began seeking a special buyer for these, one who they knew would appreciate a find such as this and pay extra to have it cut to custom specifications. It didn't take long before an Italian businessman by the name of Giovanni Puccini, a wealthy merchant and trader, expressed interest. Giovanni gave precise specifications on how he wanted the diamonds cut. Now, are either of you aware of the fact that the diamonds are not truly identical?"

Vic looked to Jones who looked back and shrugged.

"No, we weren't aware of that Al," replied Jones.

"It's a common misconception actually, that these are identical diamonds. In fact, while the diamonds are of the same size or carat, and look very similar at first glance, there is a defining difference between the two. Giovanni wanted one diamond cut with a pentagon face, so the main surface on the top of this diamond has five equal length sides. For the other diamond, he wanted it shaped into a hexagon, so the face has six sides. I won't explain why he had these cut in this unique way suffice to say that he intended them to be used in certain esoteric rituals, as a means to enhance the effects of the ritual." Al paused, sounding like he was having a drink. After a few seconds he cleared his throat. "Now, this next part is very important. Is everyone still paying attention?"

"Yes, absolutely," said Vic, he had been listening intently to Al's words. He had glanced over at Jones as well who also appeared very engaged. "Please proceed."

"Ah, very good," Al said, sounding pleased. "Now, as Giovanni continued to use these diamonds for his purposes, word had begun to spread in certain circles about their power and beauty. The world first became aware of them as the Puccini Diamonds, their original name. Unfortunately for Puccini, at the age of fifty-six he passed away unexpectedly. Doctors diagnosed it as natural causes and the diamonds passed to his two sons, one diamond for each son." Al's voice had grown softer now, his voice fervent. "Unknown to the sons, at some point during Puccini's use of the diamonds, they begun to exert certain negative traits. Now, I'm hesitant to use the word curse as I don't believe it accurately represents the power and intelligence that is now linked to these diamonds. In reality, it's more of a compulsion, or an exertion of will that emanates from the diamonds and influences the actions of man. Referred to in some circles as the Evil Eye, it's known to affect others differently. Are any of you gentlemen familiar with the term *fascination*? The ancient definition of the word."

Vic and Jones looked at each other again and shrugged, not certain where Al was going with this. "I know what it means to be fascinated with something. Is that the response you're looking for?" asked Jones.

"Well, to a certain extent. In ancient times the meaning was similar, however, someone who was fascinated by something was believed to be under a spell, or under the power of someone or something. People were believed to have the power to fascinate other people to the point that one person could control the other through a power that flows through the eyes. In some areas it was considered witchcraft to be able to control someone with a mere glance, and people who were thought, in some cases unjustly so, to have this power were hanged as witches. When a man looks lustily upon a woman he is said to be giving her an envious eye, or vice-versa, if a woman looked lustily upon a man she could be thought to be trying to exert a power over him. Many an innocent woman was hanged over nothing more than a mere glance. Over time the term came to be known as giving someone an evil eye, but always it was meant to be someone who looked upon things with envy."

"You're talking about what happened in Salem, Massachusetts right?" asked Vic.

"Precisely, though that type of thing occurred all over the world and all throughout history, especially in the Middle East. To expand on that, it was believed that objects could also be the focus of the evil eye and actually trap some of that jealous energy from people staring enviously at it. Obviously, two of the rarest, most wondrous diamonds ever to be unearthed are bound to attract an envious eye. Wouldn't you agree?"

"I'd say so," Jones stated.

"Now take that energy and the uses that Puccini had for the diamonds, and you can see how these could come to foster a sinister energy." Al paused to take another sip before continuing. "Now, it was believed that Puccini had a habit of staring at the diamonds for hours on end, and that his death came from a slow transferring of his energy to the diamonds, but that is just speculation. After his death, the diamonds passed on to his sons and unfortunately for the sons of Giovanni, it filled them with greed, jealousy, and hatred for each other. They feuded bitterly, each vying to lay claim to the other's diamond. In the end, the elder Puccini won, the younger lost with his life. The elder then disappeared and after about twenty years, his body turned up dead in a dark alleyway in New York at the turn of the twentieth century. The diamonds were never found and for a century they were missing to the world. History never forgot them and over time they became remembered, in very small circles, as the Red Diamond Eyes. It was only recently that their whereabouts had become known. The previous owner, though unwilling to divulge where he got them, paid a very handsome amount and was quite furious at their recent disappearance. I believe you know the rest of the story."

Vic was stunned as it occurred to him that he was in a predicament he wasn't sure he really wanted to be in, with powers outside of his control at play. He suddenly felt powerless and weak.

"You're telling me we are under the influence of a force called the Evil Eye?" asked Jones, incredulous.

"Perhaps that's what it began as, but over time it is also possible that dark energy, such as the kind that the diamonds feed on, can grow to the point of becoming self-aware and display intelligent thought. At the moment though, I cannot conclusively say what kind power is held within those stones," replied Al, a hint of melancholy in his voice. "I am hoping to acquire them in the hopes of studying them extensively. Now, to address the current situation. There is some help I am able to provide. I'm sending some amulets out to you, rush shipment. Keep them on your person and they will provide protection from the compulsion felt by the diamonds, protection from the

Evil Eye. Wear them around your neck at all times, touching your skin. Even when you're sleeping, that should help with the dreams."

"I'm sorry but what we experienced in the house last night was a little more than just compulsion. Footsteps upstairs when no one else was up there, unexplained cold spots, and something breathed on my neck!" Jones stated, disturbed.

"Really?" replied Al, sounding intrigued. "To the best of my knowledge I don't believe that has anything to do with the diamonds. The house may have a spirit or two still living there. I know these are *touchy* subjects, but there are dimensions and planes of existence out there that we do not see or feel like the physical one we presently occupy, however, I assure you they are out there and you must believe me when I tell you that just as there are spirits occupying places that we cannot see, the diamonds exert an influence along those same planes that affect us. You must believe this and believe in your instincts and individual power of will if you hope to overcome these forces and succeed."

"Alright, we understand," said Jones, watching Vic as he spoke.

"Gentlemen, that is all the assistance I can offer at this time. I need to drop off the call now. Dean, I'll be in touch." Al beeped off the line.

"Jones, Vic," Dean began uncertainly, "I can't begin to imagine what's going through your heads right now. Personally, I'm having a hard time believing everything I heard myself. The dreams, the activity in the house, it all sounds a little fantastical if you ask me." Dean paused for a second then gave a brief laugh. "Though, to be honest, I've known Marcus for a long time. He was very instrumental in helping me get to where I am at right now. I'm still a little upset about what happened to him in that house, but if there's the slightest chance his spirit is still there and is responsible for the activity you guys experienced. Well, I don't think he'd try to harm you guys at all and if he knows you were sent by me, maybe he'll back off and let you guys work. He was never a quitter, he always fought to win and almost always came through. I miss him."

"I got to work with him on that Vegas job," Jones began, "He was a clever guy, came through in remarkable ways on that job."

Dean laughed, "Yeah that was fucked up situation. These jobs never seem to go as planned. Well, I wanted to let you guys know I really appreciate your efforts over there and I know this must be a lot to take in but I have faith that you can make it through. I also wanted to mention that due to the circumstances, I will be upping your share in the sale of these. We'll be splitting the sale of these evenly, each getting around three-million, three-hundred-thousand dollars each. If the both of you come through on this we will all be a lot more well off gentlemen. Don't let me down."

Vic saw Jones' eyebrows rise at that, he was sure he was showing the same reaction. After one job he could be a multi-millionaire, possibly by this time next week!

"We appreciate it. We won't let you down," Jones said with confidence.

"For all our sakes, I hope your right," said Dean with a hint of trouble in his voice. "I'll be in touch. Good luck."

They heard a click then Jones' screen went black. Jones and Vic sat there for a while. Vic was trying to sort through all his thoughts and emotions, too stunned to think straight. The money was front and center in mind. He wouldn't have to do a job ever again after this. This is the kind of payoff he'd always been hoping for. He and Shelly could run off somewhere, travel the world. All they had to do was find those two diamonds.

"Damn man," said Jones, wistfully. "Three million dollars. How the hell are we gonna pull this off? We have cursed diamonds exerting an influence on us in our sleep, and maybe when we're awake too. There's a ghost fucking with us in the house that's affecting our equipment, and all we need to do us come up with two small ass diamonds."

Vic had similar thoughts running through his head.

"Hopefully whatever Al sends will help with the diamond's influence. Like he said, we're close man. We can do this. Maybe we need to strategize this a little differently."

"What do you mean?" asked Jones.

"Well for one, I think I'll head over to the local library today and see if I can find out any useful information about the house. Any history about it—floor plans, property info. It might be a long shot but maybe I'll find some clues as to a hiding spot, or maybe even why Marcus chose that particular house. Since the housing market crashed there are abandoned properties all over the place in this region. Why did he come all the way out here and hide them in this particular house?"

Jones thought about it. "I've been wondering that myself. It wouldn't hurt for you to get some more info if you can. I still need to go through the equipment and make sure all the batteries are charged and make sure everything's working. I'll see if I can come up with any other equipment that may be useful in the search. I'm not sure what else we could use just yet, especially with that *presence* there."

"I know, I've been thinking about that too," replied Vic, brow creased in thought. "Especially when Dean mentioned the notion that Marcus might be the spirit that was interacting with us." Vic thought back to that night with his girlfriend, arms wrapped around her, watching the show. He enjoyed being scared that night and believing in the unexplained.

Jones was watching him intently. "What do you got man?"

It was a long shot but it worked in the television show so there's no reason to believe it wouldn't work here. Vic Abelson's lips curled to a smile. "I have an idea."

CHAPTER 6

Circles

Jones' eyes narrowed, "I'm listening."

"When we were in the house and the crazy shit started happening, it happened around the blood stains right? Marcus's blood stains. Maybe Marcus is still there and is trying to communicate with us. Dean said he was a loyal friend. If we let him know we're on his side, maybe he'll help point us in the right direction."

Jones' head dropped, not appearing to like it at first. Then he contemplated it further.

"Another guy died too. How do we know it's not him?"

Vic hadn't considered that possibility. "I suppose it could be the other guy, or even something older from before this even happened, but that first time I bent down by the blood stains against the wall I felt that electric charge and sensed something was there. I just have this feeling that Marcus is the one interacting with us."

Jones shrugged, "Okay, even if it is him. How do we communicate with a ghost?"

"The night before I drove out here I was with my girlfriend. We were watching a show about a group of people hunting ghosts in some mental hospital. They used digital voice recorders with the mic set to the highest sensitivity level to record ghost voices, and they actually recorded responses to questions they were asking and played it back live. Some voices get picked up on these things that you can't hear with your own ears but with intelligent responses to questions. These people firmly believed they were communicating with ghosts. I'm thinking we need to bring one of those voice recorders in there and do the same. We tell the spirit that we're associates of Dean and maybe he'll tell us where the diamonds are hidden."

Jones thought about it for a second. "Well, I can't believe I'm saying this but why the hell not. We'll just ask a ghost for help."

"I'm serious man."

"I know," replied Jones. "This is just fucking odd and I don't cope with weird shit that well, but it makes sense to try. Plus it beats having one of us stick our hand down another toilet hole. We need a plan B though, in case that doesn't work. You go to the library and find out what you can. I'll get the equipment ready and pick up these voice recorders. Just try and think of some other ways to help speed up the search and thoughts on where the diamonds might be in case we don't get any supernatural assistance."

"Aright, I'll stop by later and let you know what I find out," said Vic, standing up. He needed to get out of this room anyway. Jones' odor was starting to get to him.

"Get us some good intel."

"Will do," Vic nodded to Jones in farewell and headed back to his room. Once inside, he sat down on the bed and rubbed his temples for a minute. What Al had mentioned to them was a lot to take in. Cursed diamonds, an evil eye—with three million dollars on the line he needed to focus. His head still felt groggy and sluggish so he decided to brew up some coffee while he booted up his laptop.

"Where is the library around here?" asked Vic aloud as he

sat down with cup in hand. He connected to his hotspot and VPN, opened the browser, and found that the library was actually across from the courthouse down the street, in the old reddish-brown brick building. The building itself was over one-hundred years old which led Vic to grow intrigued about the history of the town of Emerald Ash, any information about the town might give further insight into the old house.

Vic searched through the municipal website as well as Wikipedia, finding some interesting info. It was settled in 1835 in an area on the northern banks of the Kishwaukee River by mostly farmers, though it eventually became home of the county seat. Vic was also surprised to learn the town had been a known stop in the Underground Railroad prior to the Civil War. A man by the name of Jesse Kellogg had a hidden dugout under a corn granary that was used to hide slaves traveling up the Mississippi from southern states on their way to Chicago where they would board boats that travelled the Great Lakes to freedom.

Intrigued, he decided to shut down his laptop and continue his research at the library. He grabbed his wallet, keys, and jacket then headed out the door. His stomach rumbled and the coffee the motel provided didn't do much to shake his fatigue so his first stop was to a gas station to get an energy drink and some snacks.

After pulling out of the gas station he found the library easily enough, its reddish-brown bricks were easy to spot at the main intersection in town. He pulled his car into the parking lot and found a spot near a large circular section of the building left of the entrance. As he walked up Vic took time to admire the building itself which had a Roman façade around the front entrance with a circular room to his left that had a peaked roof, and the bulk of the library to his right. It reminded him of the type of building that would be found on a university campus which brought back memories of the year he went away to college and got in the habit of attending more parties than classes. Life was much easier and simple back then.

Once inside, Vic spoke with a librarian at the desk and was directed to the Joiner history room which was on the far side of the building and where he was told he could find old news clippings on file from local papers going back a hundred years or more. He walked the short winding hallway through the library and found the room, sitting down at one of the computer stations. He popped open his energy drink and gave it a long chug while contemplating what to search for first, eventually deciding to check out any news articles he could find that related to Old Forks Road or the Smith family.

An hour or two passed as Vic went through news articles and clippings going back to the late 1800's. One piece that caught his attention was an article from the local paper of that era which mentioned the Kellogg property he read about earlier but also mentioned that Foster and Smith properties were also used as stops in the Underground Railroad. It didn't directly correlate to the property on Old Forks Road but Vic couldn't rule out the possibility that there was a hidden area somewhere on that property until he found a news article stating the house itself was built in 1913, along with the floor plan as it was used by the same construction company on several houses built in the area during that timeframe. There just wasn't any spot where hidden rooms or passages could fit based on what he saw.

Vic decided to search for any documents or sale-of-land contracts but wasn't able to locate any official records with this computer. He cleared the browsing history, stood up and stretched, then decided to check with the librarian.

"Where can I find records on properties in this area?" asked Vic as he approached the front desk.

"The courthouse across the street would have detailed records on that." The nice old lady behind the desk told him.

"Of course," Vic nodded and said thanks then walked back to the computer he was using with his things, pondering whether to risk making an appearance in the courthouse and running into the Sheriff from the day before. He ended up walking to a nearby store to grab a baseball cap and give it a shot, feeling he exhausted his options at the library. He left his car in the library parking lot, crossed the street, and walked up to the entrance of the courthouse, keeping an eye out for the Sheriff from the other day.

Vic passed through the metal detector at the entrance and was directed to the records room on the first floor toward the end of the building. Vic mentioned he was an investigative reporter and a young man behind the counter was happy to help him locate records pertaining to a Smith family on Old Forks Road, and pointed him to a desk in the other room where he could look over the documents.

He had never really researched property history like this before and was surprised at how much info he was able to find. In a small matter of time he was able to identify past owners of the land and Vic was startled to find that the land was owned by a Smith family from the early 1850's up to the housing market crash a couple years ago, leaving Vic to wonder if Marcus had any connection to the home. Smith was such a common last name and he couldn't verify conclusively.

Vic noticed the sun was setting through a window in the courthouse when he received a call on his cell phone.

"Hey."

"Vic, it Jones. Where you at?"

"Uh, the courthouse, just finishing up some research."

"Really," replied Jones, surprised. "Your not running into our old friend from the other day, are you?"

"He's nowhere in sight and I'm a little incognito," replied Vic quietly, looking around to make sure no one was eavesdropping.

"Alright, listen man there's a diner down the road from the motel. Do you want to meet up there in about twenty minutes? I could go for some food."

Vic looked at the time, noting it was almost five. His stomach had been rumbling and he was pretty sure he'd searched through as much as he could at this point. "Yeah, I know the place you're talking about. I'll be there."

"Cool, see you in a bit." Vic heard the click before he could reply. He stretched, then got up from his seat, returned the documents he checked out, and walked out of the courthouse and back to the library parking lot. It was noticeably colder out as he walked and he zipped up his jacket as he crossed the street. His head was fuzzy from reading all day and he was looking forward to finally getting a good meal and fresh coffee.

He got in his car and found the diner quickly, and wasn't there long before Jones arrived. Once they were seated in a booth Jones fished around in his pocket and slid two items forward on the table. "Got some voice recorders. What do you think?"

"Those look right," replied Vic, picking one up and having a look at it. "Let's hope they come through for us."

"Yeah," replied Jones. "It's a pretty big long shot if you ask me though. Talking ghosts, shit. I'll believe it when I hear it."

A week ago Vic would have said the same thing, but after what happened in the house the other night he was willing to believe. "You get anything else?"

Jones shook his head, "No, I'm getting everything ready to go though. Batteries are charging. We'll be set to rollout at dark tomorrow."

Vic nodded and they paused as a young and pretty waitress approached to fill up their coffee and take their order. After she left they leaned closer.

"Did you find anything out about the house?" asked Jones before taking a sip of coffee.

"I found out it was owned by a Smith family up until a few years ago. Marcus' last name is Smith. Any chance he's related to whoever owned the house?"

Jones considered it for a moment. "I suppose it's possible, I know he was from the Midwest. Smith a pretty common name though."

Vic nodded in agreement, "Yeah, it's worth considering. I also found some interesting history about the town and the house but nothing really helpful in zeroing in on a location for the diamonds. The house was built in 1913 and has a common floor plan to others in the area. No obvious hiding spots that I saw though."

Jones appeared thoughtful, "Yeah, that house isn't very big to be hiding a secret room or anything. That's interesting information though."

Vic took a sip of coffee, appreciating the flavor much more than the crap the motel provided. "You think these amulet's Al is sending will do anything?"

Jones shrugged, uncertain. "Your guess is as good as mine."

Vic nodded and continued to sip his coffee, finally enjoying some time to relax. "I hope they work. I need to get some restful sleep." The stress of the last couple days and lack of sleep were taking a toll. He could feel it along with the jitters of being strung out on caffeine and energy drinks.

Jones nodded in agreement, "So what are you going to do when you get back? You gonna try and sleep, or stay awake?"

"Stay awake," replied Vic without hesitation. The dreams from earlier still drifted into his thoughts on occasion. The prison with the long line of prisoners, the padded room with the eyes and the serpent, he still pictured those dreams clearly in his mind.

"Me too," said Jones. His eyes were distant.

The sound of thunder rumbled overhead and Jones' eyes locked with his. Vic had checked the weather earlier and knew a thunderstorm was forecast to come through along with steady rain from a cold front passing through the area, one more reason they didn't want to go back to the house tonight. Vic and Jones continued to look at each other and Vic finally broke the silence. "I know that we're not supposed to know much about each other but I'm curious how long you have known Dean, you two seem pretty close."

Jones starred back at him for a moment then shrugged, "I suppose it wouldn't hurt to say a few things. Dean and I go back over ten years now, back before he took over the business. We worked a job together, sufficed to say it got hairy and we both helped each other get through it." Jones took a sip from his coffee, distant gaze returning. "He saved my life. I saved his," Jones paused for a second then laughed. "He hated me at first, I was arrogant and proud. I didn't really warm up to him right away either, he was too preachy and I felt he viewed me like a kid. But that's how it is sometimes at the start of a friendship, sometimes you start out at odds then find out that you accentuate each other's differences and together you make a good team."

Vic smirked, "Yeah, I can relate to that." Jones smiled in agreement. Lightning flashed outside and thunder rolled as both Jones and Vic looked up, hearing raindrops hit the ceiling above.

"Dean once told me that life moves in circles," Jones began. "You have your ups and downs, you make forward progress in your life, sometimes you fall back. Throughout it all there are times where you feel like you fell back to where you started from, however long ago." Jones took another sip of coffee then leaned forward. "I'm not saying this like it's a bad thing, but I've been feeling that way about this job. After all the jobs I've done before, here I am again, with another fresh face and the promise of wealth ahead of me, with a seemingly impossible task to overcome in order to achieve it. When does it end?"

Vic shrugged, leaning forward. "It ends when you break the cycle. I think we have a shot of doing that now. Yes, we're here, doing another job. But if we finish this the payout is enough to break any cycle. We come through and we're both set for life, no more taking chances on promises of wealth, we'll have the wealth to move forward, and keep moving forward. There will be no having to go back after this."

Jones still looked distant, "And what if we don't come through?"

That thought had been running through Vic's mind but he pushed those negative feelings away. The first step in any goal you set is to believe in yourself. Vic firmly felt that once you believe in yourself you can achieve anything. "I'm not willing to accept that possibility. We have the greatest opportunity of our lives in front of us." Vic leaned forward, speaking softly but intently. "Like Al said, with all this weird stuff going on that can only mean the diamonds are in that house, and since they're there, we'll find them. We'll break the cycle."

Jones grinned, nodding as he leaned in closer, "I'm with you. We're not leaving here empty handed!"

"Hell yes," replied Vic, feeling energized. Lightning flashed and thunder rumbled outside but that did nothing to diminish their mood. Both of them stared out the window contemplating their job when the waitress arrived with their food, placing it down in front of them then refilled their coffee.

"Let me know if you boys need anything else," she stated with a smile. Vic caught Jones checking out her ass as she walked away.

"There's definitely something else I need from her," said Jones before he turned his attention back to his food.

Vic felt the waitress might have been a little young but just smirked and began devouring the food on his plate. They both ate in silence as the rain continued to pour down, each finishing their meal within a couple minutes. After clearing their plates and pushing them aside, they waited for the check.

"Wow, you guys must have been hungry," the waitress said as she approached and took their plates. "Anything else I can get you?"

Jones looked her up and down and spoke in a deep voice, "Yeah, what time do you get off work?"

Vic choked as he took a sip of coffee, shocked by Jones' actions. The waitress looked startled then stood up straight with the plates in her hand. "I'm here until close then my boyfriend will be picking me up," she replied curtly.

"We'll just take the check," Vic interjected. The waitress looked at him for a second and walked off. Vic looked to Jones who was eying him with a disapproving look. "What's that about? We need to be low-key here."

Jones just shrugged nonchalantly and looked back toward the waitress. She returned with the check, and without sparing a glance at Jones, laid it down on the table and quickly walked away. Jones eyed her the whole time.

"I got it," offered Vic, grabbing the check off the table. Jones grunted something incoherent but got up and grabbed his coat.

"I need to pick up a few more things. I'll see you tomorrow," Jones murmured then walked out of the diner. Vic watched as he left then went to pay the bill, apologizing to the waitress as she rung him up. Jones had left by the time Vic walked into the parking lot.

Knowing he was in for a long night, Vic made another stop at the gas station for energy drinks and snacks for the night. The rain had lessened to a drizzle and a nearly full moon rose from the horizon when Vic pulled back into the parking lot of the Main Street Inn. He looked for Jones' Caddy but didn't see it in any of the spots. Vic hoped Jones wasn't too upset with him for interjecting but supposed he would find out tomorrow. He fumbled for the keys to his room but managed to get them out and open the door.

Once inside, he put his bags down and pulled his phone out of his pocket, letting out a breath when he viewed a pic Shelly had text him of her standing naked and dripping wet in the shower with a towel barely covering her.

I'M GETTING WET THINKING OF YOU, the text below the picture read, which made Vic laugh-out-loud. He spent a minute or two thinking of a reply.

YOU'RE MAKING IT VERY HARD, TO BE AWAY FROM YOU, he text back.

Vic put his phone down then turned on the television and began flipping through the channels, not finding anything interesting to watch. Thoughts of Shelly ran through his mind, making him smile. He felt lucky to have found her, comparing her to be just as rare as one of the diamonds they were searching for. It left him wondering how he would tell her the true reason he left this week, that he had just became a multi-millionaire. Could he tell her that he was a thief hunting stolen diamonds? Would she care how he came by the money?

His phone buzzed again and Vic was pleased to see more pics, making him truly rock-hard. With nothing better to do Vic decided to join Shelly and began pleasuring himself to the pics on his phone. It didn't take long before he was grabbing tissues to clean up.

He lay in bed and continued to flip through channels. Time passed and he caught himself about to doze off after a while and got out of bed to crack another energy drink. It was only nine o'clock and he didn't want to burn through them but one was definitely needed right now. Vic flipped through channels most of the night, doing things to help stay awake. He worked out for a bit doing jumping jacks, then pushups and sit ups followed by some stretching. It helped for a while but as the night wore on a strong weariness set in and the energy drinks he consumed only seemed to fuel a strong headache.

Shortly before two in the morning Vic caught himself about to doze off again and got out of bed, finding he was out of energy drinks. He walked to the bathroom and splashed cold water on his face. As he looked into the mirror two red, bloodshot eyes stared back at him with dark circles underneath. His head pounded. Rain continued to pour down outside and lightning flashed as he walked back and laid on the bed. He stared blankly at the screen as he flipped through channels, cycling through them over and over repeatedly, well into the night.

CHAPTER 7

Dreams

Darkness filled his vision as he ascended the basement stairs. Most of the treads creaked and some wobbled under his feet with each step. Fear made his heart pound, though he wasn't entirely sure where he was or why he was afraid. He reached a short landing at the top of the stairs and felt around with his left hand, searching for a door. His fingers brushed against a circular knob and closed around it, giving it a turn. Slowly, he pulled open the door as a shrill creak emitted from its rusty hinges. The faintest of light shone through the doorway, and Sheriff Eli Hurth stepped through into a hallway.

A sudden noise caught his attention, off to his left, and he froze, remaining still and silent. The sinking feeling at the bottom of his stomach swelled, its icy fingers stretching further through his insides but Eli survived much worse places than this and learned to suppress that fear and do his job.

What is my job? What am I doing here?

He remained motionless while pondering these questions when another unexpected noise to his left disrupted his train of thought. It was closer this time. Footsteps, slowly approaching. His heart pumped faster and louder in his chest as he looked in the direction of the footsteps, not seeing anyone approach.

Frantically, he reached down to his side, searching for the flashlight that clung to his belt, wondering why he hadn't grabbed it earlier. His fingers wrapped around the cold metal and he pulled it loose and pointed it toward the noise.

Upon flicking the power switch, Eli was shocked when a deep red luminescence shot forth. This wasn't the kind of light he was expecting. *Why is this red*? He didn't have time to think about that as he looked down a hallway with decaying walls and a boarded up entryway, making a startling realization. It was *the* house, with the double homicide he investigated a few weeks ago.

"What's going on?" he called out, confused.

Silence answered him. The footsteps ceased. His heart beat so hard in his chest it almost hurt. He looked around, not seeing anything other than the peeling walls of the old house. Eli took a step forward, the old oak hardwood boards creaking as he transitioned weight to his forward foot, very similar to the sound of footsteps he just heard. He continued forward as the hallway opened up to an arched entryway with a room on his right. Panning the flashlight across the room, his gaze traced along the walls to a boarded up window, on what would have been the front of the property, to the adjacent side of the room where he gasped to see a body sitting motionless against the wall under another boarded up window. Its head was slumped over and body motionless. A dark liquid glistened in a pool around it.

"Who's there?" Eli's voice faltered as he spoke. With his free hand, he reached for the gun in his belt holster. "This is Sheriff Eli Hurth, identify yourself."

A gurgling noise came from the body as its head began

to rise, revealing a decaying face and glowing eyes. Eli's hands began to shake as he realized the eyes were reflecting back the red of the flashlight in his hand. It was disturbingly breathtaking and he became transfixed on its eyes as they locked onto his.

The body lurched forward and began to rise from the dark pool that surrounded it, blood came oozing out of its mouth and the glowing eyes remained locked with his, continually reflecting a kaleidoscope of red. It stood up and raised its arms forward and began creeping towards him. Eli tried to lift his arm and bring his gun up to fire, but his arm wouldn't move. He tried to take a step back, but his legs wouldn't respond to his commands. Eli could only look on in terror as his body froze, paralyzed.

The decaying body drew near, its hands stretching out for the Sheriff's throat. Eli tried putting his hands up to block it, to do something, but he just stood there. All he could do was stare into those hideous eyes, its glimmering aura filling Eli's vision until he saw nothing but a million shades of red. Ice cold fingers wrapped around his throat.

Sheriff Eli Hurth finally managed to let out a long, horrid scream.

"Wake up, honey, wake up," a voice spoke with urgency. Something was shaking him. He opened his eyes, relieved to find they were greeted by the concerned eyes of his wife, whose dark brown locks of hair fell still as she stopped shaking him and appearing relieved at his revival.

"I'm up, I'm up," said Eli, groggily. His heart was still pounding. "What's the matter? What happened?"

His wife's eyes still shone with concerned. "You were having a bad dream or something. You were shuffling about in bed then you let out a horrific scream. It scared me to death. Are you alright?"

He pictured he was in the house, unable to move. He fought down the fear that lingered and struggled to get a grip on himself. "I just had a bad dream honey, it's alright. What time is it?" He looked around for the clock.

"It's three-thirty in the morning," she replied.

It was still about an hour before he got up normally, but Eli decided he didn't want to go back to sleep so he threw the covers over and got out of bed. "I think I'm going to put on some coffee and get into work a little early."

His wife seemed like she was about to protest but he just walked out of the room, leaving her confused as to what was going on. He'd only been in the house a couple times before, but he knew where that dream had taken place, a house that had been on his mind a lot lately. The events that happened there— the deaths, the haunting feeling of being watched whenever he was there, the strangers from the other day. It was all that was on his mind lately. The stress of it seemed to be taking a toll yet he couldn't shake the feeling that something was going down there, something big, and that he needed to get to the bottom of it.

❊ ❊ ❊

Vic shot up in his bed, suddenly awoken from a vivid dream. He glanced at the alarm clock, its red digital numbers displayed 03:33 a.m. Rain poured down outside and a flash of lightning lit up the window. Vic got out of bed and went to make a pot of coffee with the last pouch of filtered grounds the motel provided. It was another disturbing dream, this time in the house itself.

What was the Sheriff doing there?

Vic pondered this as the coffee brewed. The dream started normal enough, he was in the house searching for the diamonds when he heard someone coming up the basement stairs. Startled, and knowing Jones was upstairs on the second floor, he crept back toward the kitchen and watched from the darkness as the Sheriff who helped them out the other day walked out of the basement and into the hallway. Something caught the Sheriff's attention toward the front of the house and Vic continued to watch as the Sheriff slowly moved down the hall to investigate. He walked into the living room on the right and Vic was about to go follow him when he heard a horrid scream and woke up. *Weird,* Vic thought.

He sat down in the chair next to the desk with the coffee maker and slapped his face to wake up a bit more. His head was still groggy and he had a strong urge to lay back down while the coffee brewed.

"What the fuck is going on?" he asked aloud to no-one in particular.

Vic checked his phone to see if he missed any calls or texts from Shelly but nothing came through so he checked his email and social media. When the coffee finished brewing he threw his phone on the bed and poured himself a cup. Normally, he took his coffee with an overly generous helping of sugar, but all Vic had left in the room was low calorie sweetener. He read too many articles about the negative side effects of those so he just drank it black. It was bitter, stale, and excessively hot, but after a sipping on it for a few minutes he was finally able to keep his eyelids from feeling like they were heavy garage doors about to slam shut.

He sat in the chair and watched television for a while, flipping between the countless infomercials and thoughtless shows that plagued the screen at this hour of the morning. When he managed to find a show that caught his interest it quickly ended and was followed by an advertisement for a miracle cooking utensil, or some new dating service. At around six in the morning he started watching the news only to find that it was filled with nothing but depressing stories involving stupid people. It made his mood sour. The pot of coffee had run dry and Vic's eyelids had begun to droop again as he continued to watch morning shows filled with plucky people discussing the days events. It was a quarter to nine when his phone started buzzing. Vic got up and grabbed it off the bed and saw Jones' number.

"Hey," said Vic as he brought the phone to his ear. After they parted at the diner, Vic got the impression that Jones wasn't too pleased with him. He hoped that Jones had gotten over him speaking up for the waitress.

"Hey Vic," Jones began wearily. He paused for a moment before continuing. "First off, you were right last night. I was out of line with that waitress, if they had called the police and that Sheriff arrived that wouldn't have been good. Just been cooped up alone in this damn motel too long."

That was a relief to Vic, "It's cool man, no harm done."

"Alright," said Jones, sounding slightly relieved. "On a brighter note, I did just receive a priority package via early morning delivery. Al paid almost two-hundred dollars to have these amulets shipped out so quickly. Come by whenever to pick yours up, I'll be here."

That was what Vic wanted to hear. He wasn't sure how much longer he could have put off sleep. His eyelids were heavy and his eyes burned. "Nice, I'll head over now."

Vic didn't bother washing his face or cleaning up at all, he grabbed his room key and walked out the door then made the quick stroll that separated his room from Jones' and gave a knock on room 113. Jones answered quickly, his eyes were sunken in and Vic noticed the familiar, foul odor emanating from Jones that he, unfortunately, was getting used to.

"You look like shit," said Vic with a smirk. "Though probably still looking better than I do."

Jones grunted and held up the package that just arrived. It was a wide express envelope that was about an inch thick. Jones reached in and pulled out its contents, which were thoroughly encased in cardboard and bubble-wrap, and handed one to Vic who turned it around, trying to figure out where to open it from. Vic found the piece of tape holding it all together and tore it apart and unwrapped it, finding a small circular item inside, about the size of a teacup saucer. It was made of half-inch thick blown glass that was solid blue on the perimeter, white inside of that, and black in the middle. On the outer edge of the glass was a small loop hole, making it appear the item was meant to be worn as a necklace. Vic realized that overall it looked like a blue eyeball.

"There's this note too," said Jones, handing over a piece of paper to Vic.

WEAR THIS ON YOU AT ALL TIMES. IDEALLY AROUND YOUR NECK, TOUCHING YOUR SKIN. GOOD LUCK GENTLE-MEN.

-AL

Vic had doubts about whether this thing would work, but after what they'd been experiencing lately he was definitely going to give it a shot.

"I'm thinking we head out shortly after sundown tonight," Jones said firmly. "Let's meet here around six-thirty. Be ready to go. We finish this tonight." Jones looked weary, but there was an intense determination in his eyes.

Vic nodded and carefully placed his amulet in his pocket. He looked to Jones, expecting more, but Jones stared back blankly. "I'd love to have you stay and chat, have a delightful conversation over some tea," said Jones sarcastically, "but I'm about to crash. Please get the fuck out."

Vic smirked and turned toward the door.

"Sweet dreams," Vic called out as he left.

Vic breathed in the cool air as he walked back to his room. It had stopped raining shortly after sunrise and there was a crispness to the air that always lingered after a good downpour. When he got to his door he paused, realizing he wanted to enjoy being outside for a second. After spending all night indoors, he decided a little more fresh air before napping might help.

He reached into his pocket and pulled out the amulet, its surface reflecting the morning sunlight in his eyes. *An eye to protect me from an eye. This is too crazy.* Another light reflected in his eyes, coming from the street the motel was on. It reflected off the red surface of the lights mounted atop a police cruiser that slowly passed by. It looked like the Sheriff's vehicle as it passed. Vic took one last breath of fresh air and opened the door to his room.

Inside, Vic took off his shoes and fell back on the bed. His head pounded and he felt tense, probably from all the caffeine and lack of sleep. The amulet was in his hands, he slipped it under his shirt and held it to his chest. It felt cool at first but began to warm up. The long night had taken its toll and it wasn't long before Vic's breathing slowed, and sleep took him.

Vic opened his eyes.

It was dark in the room. Everything was still and silent. His hands were folded over each other against his chest, cupping the amulet beneath. He rolled over and checked the alarm clock, it read 06:09 p.m.

"Shit," he cursed under his breath. Seeing as how he was supposed to meet up with Jones in twenty minutes, that didn't leave him much time to get ready. He quickly got out of bed, forgetting he had the amulet which fell through his shirt to the floor. Vic felt a surge of panic before he saw it laying in one piece on the soft carpet by his feet. Relieved, he grabbed it off the floor and placed it on the table in plain sight. That was not something he wanted to forget.

He grabbed some clothes out of his suitcase and walked to the bathroom. After a long refreshing piss, he hopped in the shower and turned the water on hot. It burned slightly, but Vic liked it that way, either really hot or really cold. Steam had filled the bathroom and Vic's skin was pink by the time he finished and hopped out. He grabbed a fresh towel and quickly dried himself off. Condensation fogged up the mirror as he went to comb his hair but he managed to slick back his hair and brush his teeth without seeing his reflection.

After the shower he grabbed some clothes, deciding on his lucky white fleece as he was going to need all the luck he could get tonight. After he slid the fleece over his head he checked the time, it was still a couple minutes before he had to meet up with Jones. He looked around the room and found the duffel bag with all his gear. Luckily, he left that packed from yesterday so that was ready to go. He grabbed his guns and slid the twin-leather holsters around his arms.

The amulet lay on the table and Vic looked around the room, searching for something to hang it from. It dawned on him that Shelly had given him a rosary necklace before he left. *Another form of charm,* he thought. Vic searched his suitcase and eventually pulled out the silver chain necklace. He undid the clasp at the back and quickly realized that the cross was hard fixed to the chain and wouldn't slide off.

I suppose two charms are better than one.

He grabbed the amulet and slid it on the chain, its hoop slid perfectly over the beaded necklace and fell in place next to the crucifix. Then he placed it around his neck and took a moment to get the clasp secure. He looked at the amulet one last time and slid it under his shirt, feeling its cool surface against his chest. It was a little heavy but he felt good wearing it. He quickly grabbed all his things and headed out the door, noting it was a little past six thirty.

Vic's stomach grumbled as he walked to Jones' room but aside from an empty stomach, he realized he was feeling much better. His head wasn't as groggy as it had been lately and he felt light on his feet as he walked. The amulet gently swayed back a forth with each step like a ticking pendulum. Maybe this thing was working already. After all, he just slept about eight hours straight without any disturbing dreams, and he felt more energized and refreshed than he had in a long time. When he reached room 113, he gave a hard knock on the door. Jones opened, his cellphone pressed against the side of his face.

"Yeah," said Jones to whoever was in the phone while he nodded at Vic to come in. He opened the door wider so Vic could clear through with his duffel bag. "That should do it for me. Hold on, my friend just walked in. Let me see if he wants anything." Jones removed the phone from his ear, "You hungry?"

"Yes," Vic replied hastily. "What kind of food?"

"Grill type food—burgers, sandwiches, pizza. The place you ordered from before."

"Nice, let me get an Italian beef, fries, and a pizza puff."

"Alright," said Jones, then he finished placing the order.

Vic looked around and saw that the room was not much better off than when he left earlier. Things were still strewn about though a few things were organized, and Jones was clean and actually smelling good for a change.

"Afraid I overslept," said Jones, looking around as he put his phone in his pocket. "Just got up about twenty minutes ago."

Vic smirked at Jones. "No worries, me too. Was going to see if you wanted to grab some food on the way but looks like I showed up at the right time."

Jones grunted, "Ah, so you rushed over here only to find that I'm running late. Aren't we supposed to be professionals? People who execute a plan according to the plan's schedule?"

Vic liked to think of himself as a professional, but in reality this was only his fifth job. So far he found that in all the jobs he's done, the original plan that was put together never seemed to hold through anyway. There's always something that happens leading to a need for improvisation. In this case, with the diamonds affecting them and the paranormal activity in the house, adapting so those things work for them seemed to be the only option. "Do things ever really go as planned in our line of work?"

Jones snorted, apparently liking Vic's reply, "No, I suppose not. Now a good plan is the foundation of a successful job, but being able to adapt that plan as circumstances change is the key to successfully finishing the job."

"I think we've adapted well so far," replied Vic. "Considering our circumstances."

"I think so too," Jones said in agreement. "Just think, in less than twelve hours we could be wealthier than either of us ever dreamed, and I know I have been dreaming of an opportunity like this for years." Jones looked away, reflective. "I sometimes forget that those dreams could actually happen, with the clutter that is my life." Jones looking around the room then back to Vic with a certain fervor in his eyes. "But I feel it now more than ever. I normally don't talk like this but I've been feeling like we were meant for this job, like some higher power is at play. The things we've been experiencing lately have only opened my mind to countless possibilities that abound in this world. I feel that good things are headed our way. Tonight we break the circle!"

Vic was about to reply when his stomach rumbled and he just looked down and laughed. "I'm hungry for what's to come tonight."

"Well hang tight," replied Jones. "Food should be here in a half hour. I'm gonna finish getting ready."

Jones shuffled about the room, cleaning up and organizing things in his big duffel bag as Vic watched the news on television. The weather forecast popped up and Vic noted that the night should be calm and clear but cold, a welcome change to the shifting weather from the past few days. They waited in the room without engaging in much conversation when a knock sounded at the door after a short time.

"Got a food delivery for room 113," a young man stated after Jones opened the door. Vic looked over to see a kid who looked like he was just out of high school who tried to grow a beard but only managed crops of patchy fuzz on his face.

"Of course," Jones stated, taking the food and a two-liter of soda and handing the bags to Vic. "Here you go, keep the change," said Jones as he gave the delivery driver a folded handful of bills. Jones then shut the door before the deliveryman could reply.

Vic cleared a spot off the table and placed the two packages down, opening one up. Steam rose from the bag and Vic's mouth watered when the aroma caught his nose. His stomach growled. Jones grabbed two Styrofoam coffee cups and began filling them from the two liter of cola. When the cups were full he handed one to Vic.

"To breaking the circle," said Jones, holding up his cup. There was an intense determination in his eyes.

Vic looked back at Jones and lifted his cup in the air. "To breaking the circle." They tapped cups and then each drank down a large gulp of soda. Vic was grateful for the cool liquid, he hadn't noticed how dry his mouth had been. His lips had been on the verge of cracking.

"This one looks like mine," Vic stated as he opened one of the bags then handed the other one to Jones which had a double cheeseburger, fries, and some other individually fried food in there. "What do I owe you?"

"Don't worry about it," replied Jones as he grabbed his bag and reached in.

They both ate heartily and hurriedly, both noting they were running way later than planned. Still, the food tasted like some of the best Vic had eaten in his life and wolfed down the beef and fries in a matter of minutes, then bit into the pizza puff as he still felt hungry and proceeded to consume that even though he initially planned on saving it for later that night. No more than ten minutes had passed and both Vic and Jones were letting out a deep breath and staring at the empty wrappers in front of them, satisfied they were stuffed to the brim.

"Alright," began Jones as he crunched up the used food wrappers and placed them in the bag, "We've wasted enough time. We're fed, we're full, now let's finish this."

"Agreed," said Vic as he cleaned up his side of the table, starting to feel a little uncomfortable from all the food he had eaten. One of the informercials he watched last night while he was trying to stay awake in the motel room popped into his mind. It discussed livestock being fed and plumped while getting ready for slaughter, they called these livestock finishers. Vic suddenly felt that he and Jones had just become finishers for tonight, fattened and ready for slaughter. He tried to shake the feeling as best he could but he walked out of Jones' room in a much less energized state than when he entered, weary for what the night held in store.

Part II

FULL MOON

...IF YOU GAZE LONG ENOUGH INTO AN ABYSS,

the abyss will gaze back into you.

-Friedrich Nietzsche

CHAPTER 8

Hunters

C rystal Diaz peered out of her second story window and smiled, seeing the full moon had finally risen from the horizon. She walked back to her desk and grabbed the items she wanted to charge: moldavite, rose quartz, smokey quartz, celestite, golden flourite, amethyst, onyx, tiger's eye, and labradorite.

"Soak it up my lovelies," she whispered as she carefully placed the crystals in a row along the windowsill, making sure each would be in direct view of the moonlight when it rose higher in a few hours. Satisfied her pieces were going to get a good charge, she grabbed the scrying mirror off her bed and stared into its dark surface, reflecting back her inquisitive eye's.

Tonight was the night she had been waiting for. When her friends asked her how she wanted to celebrate her eighteenth birthday, she immediately knew. Just like the items she carefully placed on her windowsill that bear her namesake, Crystal didn't want to have what could be considered a normal birthday celebration. She had always been drawn to the other side, the mystical side of our universe—the side behind the veil—and she planned a while back to postpone her birthday celebration to after her actual birthday, which was earlier this week, to tonight when the moon was full.

Staring into the scrying mirror, she noticed her eyes appeared sunken and hollow, her skin corpse-like. The black surface of the mirror sometimes made her appear like she was dying, but that was a common thing when scrying and she tried to look past that for any sign of what the night may hold. After a couple minutes of not seeing anything, she set the mirror back on her bed, dispirited.

She walked over to her desk and stared in her normal dresser mirror, making sure her makeup and hair still looked right. Bangs with blue-dyed tips and black roots parted from the right and hung just past her cheek covering her left eye, she stared with her right which was thick with dark eyeliner that matched her black lipstick. She wore a dark grey fleece with the flower of life pattern in purple across her chest, and black yoga pants. She grabbed her blush off the table and applied a little more to add just the right level of mystery to her appearance. Once satisfied that her makeup and hair were just right she looked into the mirror one last time and winked at herself. She grabbed her cellphone from the desk and checked the time, it would still be an hour or so before her friends showed up.

A flutter of excitement hit, she had been waiting all month for this night and it was finally here! Her two best friends would join her on a moonlit excursion to the old abandoned house down the road where they would seek out spirits in an attempt to communicate with the other side. They had already spent a few hours in the house last week and experienced activity that none of her friends could explain. Tonight, she felt like a hunter in search of more. What they experienced last time was just a teaser for what could potentially happen on a night like tonight, under a full moon.

She tried her best to quell her nervous excitement. With nothing else to do for the next hour she grabbed her scrying mirror off the bed and got lost in the dark reflections staring back at her, wondering who they would end up making contact with tonight, and what she and her friends would experience.

* * *

The full moon hung low in the sky in front of them, its faint glow illuminating the rolling cornfields that stretched out around them, as if leading them to their final destination. Stars speckled the sky around the moon, though not all that many considering how clear a night it was. Light pollution from Chicago and the western suburbs crept out this far, blocking many of the wonders of the night sky. Vic had a finger in his mouth as he gazed out the passenger window of Jones' Caddy, trying to pry loose a small chunk of food that wedged itself in a crevice between two teeth. He wasn't having any luck getting it out. It was annoying.

"The temperature dropped a good bit but at least we have a nice night for a change," said Jones as he drove. "The wind died down, hopefully the house won't be as creaky."

Vic took his finger out of his mouth, resigned to let the food stay there for now. "I have a feeling it will still be creaky."

Jones grunted in agreement but didn't say more. He had been mostly quiet since they finished eating and left the motel. Vic had been too for that matter, still unnerved by the correlation he made before leaving but he tried to clear the negative thoughts from his head. After all, it was finally time to get back to work and see this job through. Tonight required his full attention and resourcefulness.

When they came upon the spot, Jones flicked the lights off and pulled off the road, parking behind the same bushes that hid their car last time. Vic was greeted by near freezing temperatures when he opened the door and stepped out. He pulled a pair of gloves and a beanie out from his coat pocket and put them on, thankful he remembered to dress warmly this time. Jones got out and walked around back, popping the trunk. They grabbed their gear and headed toward the creek that led them to the house.

Moonlight helped guide their way, its pale glow reflecting off small puddles of standing water that remained in spots from the previous night's downpour. It was muddy and slick again and Vic already felt it build up on his shoes but did his best to keep his footing as they maneuvered around areas where water had built up or where the ground looked mushy, doing their best to stay on dry earth.

"So what's the matter, you've been pretty quiet lately?" asked Jones after a few minutes as they ducked under the branches of a hawthorn tree along their path.

"Just trying to get my head in the game," replied Vic, hoping he sounded believable. It wasn't entirely a lie, he just didn't feel like opening up now. He *was* trying to get his head in the game, after all. "If things go right tonight, tomorrow morning I'll be much more talkative."

"I hear that," replied Jones. They continued on in silence broken only by crickets and other wildlife that buzzed in the night around them.

Vic spent a good amount of time watching the sky as they hiked. When he was a kid he would spend hours outside just lying on the ground with his eyes toward the heavens, letting his mind try and comprehend the enormity of the universe and the multitude of stars, planets, and anything else that occupied our universe. As he gazed up, he made out the crooked W that formed Cassiopeia. Polaris shined in the northeast along with the Little Dipper which hung upside down. On the horizon (not in view at the moment, but he knew it was there) was the hunter Orion. As the night wore on Orion would rise higher in the sky. Vic felt like a hunter tonight. While his prey did not hide in the prairie grass, swim in a creek or float in a pond, it was something very similar—something alive. It had its own energy. Vic could feel it.

It didn't seem to take quite as long as last time before they came upon the barn that marked their destination, its old wooden panels eerily illuminated under the light of the moon. They paused at the end of a growth of wildlife that bordered the property to investigate the area. Jones reached into his duffel bag and, while making an excessive amount of noise for Vic's taste, took out his night vision goggles which he pulled over his head. Vic waited as Jones surveyed the area, giving the all-clear after a small wait. Jones rushed toward the barn, crouching as he approached the crumbling old stones that made its foundation. Vic followed close behind, eyeing their flank. They proceeded much like last time, sneaking up to the corner of the barn, scouting the area ahead then moving forward once getting the all clear. Before long, Vic and Jones were crouched by the basement window of the house. Jones pulled off the night vision goggles.

"This is it," Jones began urgently, breathe steaming as he spoke. His voice was quiet yet determined. "Let's go in there and do whatever it takes to get those diamonds. We finish this tonight!"

Vic nodded in enthused agreement. "Whatever it takes."

Jones held up his hand. Vic clasped it, locking their thumbs together while giving it a firm shake.

"Let's finish this!"

* * *

A buzzing on the bed next to her broke her concentrated gaze from the scrying mirror and she blinked a few times and looked around, her eyes focusing back to the normal view of her room. *That was odd*, she thought as she placed the mirror back on the bed and grabbed her phone. It was as if her eyes had started glowing red for a minute. That never happened before but she realized she had been staring at that thing for at least a half hour and brushed it off as her eyes playing tricks. A surge of joy and excitement hit as she read the text message she just received.

WE'RE HERE BIRTHDAY GIRL!

Crystal rushed out of her room and flew down the stairs to let her friends in. After months of planning and waiting, the time had finally come! She unlocked the front door and let it glide open as she threw her hands in the air.

"Happy birthday," her friends shouted in unison with broad smiles.

"Oh, thank you both so much," replied Crystal earnestly as she gave big hugs and invited them inside. "You both mean so much to me and I couldn't think of anyone else I'd want to celebrate my eighteenth birthday with."

Frankie smiled, she had been Crystals best friend since kindergarten. "You know we wouldn't miss it!" She had long hair that had been died purple a while back so it was faded and had blond roots exposed. She was short and plump, but undeniably looked cute with the natural-toned cosmetics she wore. Her brown eyes glowed with excitement, Frankie was just as interested in the metaphysical as her, and was looking forward to tonight with the same level of enthusiasm.

"Oh, you look fabulous honey," said Ryan as they hugged. Ryan was tall, thin, and queer. He wore a bedazzled sweater with skin-tight jeans and had eyebrows that were probably more carefully manicured than her own. She had only known Ryan (who pronounces his name Ree-Anne) for a couple years but the three of them had been inseparable lately. "Is your Abuela home?"

"No, she has to work tonight," replied Crystal.

Ryan grinned and pulled out a bottle of clear liquid along with a little baggie with fat green buds inside. "These should make for good offerings, right? We'll still have plenty for ourselves too."

"Yes," Crystal proclaimed in agreement, appreciating the orange hairs she could see in the buds. Ryan always came through with the good stuff! "What's in the bottle? Have a seat and warm up for a bit, I still need to get my things together."

"Moonshine my dad makes. You may want to grab some juice to mix it with if it's too strong," replied Ryan as he walked over and sat down on the couch in the living room while Crystal ran back upstairs to grab her things. She already had the Ouija board in her backpack so she grabbed her scrying mirror off her bed, wrapped it in a thick sweater, and placed it inside as well. She also grabbed a piece of hematite, black onyx, and her favorite crystal—a super seven, also known as a melody stone, off her desk and placed those in her pocket, immediately feeling less anxious about the tonight and more relaxed. She went to her closet and grabbed the remaining things: candles and a lighter, two flashlights with fresh batteries, and a blanket in case it got too cold again.

"Hey, do you have any plastic cups," Ryan called out from downstairs. "I forgot to bring some."

"Yeah, they're on top of the fridge," Crystal yelled back. She checked herself in the mirror one last time before heading downstairs, approving of her outfit for the night. Her backpack bulged full with everything inside but she picked it up and slid her arms through the straps and went downstairs.

"There's a bag of food by fridge as well," said Crystal as she met back up with Ryan in the kitchen. You can put those in there. There's a couple pineapple juice cans in there too."

"Mmm, looks like someone has a sweet tooth tonight," Ryan jested as he put the cups in the bag and grabbed it off the counter. "You have been planning this for a while, haven't you."

Frankie walked in, looking like she was feeling left out of the conversation. "Anything I can help with?"

"Here," stated Ryan, giving her the bag with food and cups in it. "I'll have to lug that bottle all the way there don't want to wear myself out on the way." Ryan said that last part with a flourish that made Crystal and Frankie laugh out loud.

Crystal and her friends put their gloves, hats, and winter coats back on and headed out to their destination, feeling merry and carefree as they walked under the gray light of the full moon.

✳ ✳ ✳

Vic pried open the boarding on the basement window along the edge, careful as it was about to come loose, then laid it against the foundation wall. Jones lowered himself in.

"You should be able to keep a lookout from inside this time," said Jones.

Vic nodded and lowered himself in, then reached out and replaced the boarding over the window. They were surrounded by darkness, Vic's hearing seemed more sensitive in the dark yet it was a little too quiet to be honest. No wind howled outside like last time, pressing against the house and stressing the nails and screws that held the old wood together. The background noises he'd been accustomed to were few and far between now. Vic could hear Jones' heavy breathing but that was about it. No boards creaked above and, thankfully, no footsteps were heard either.

"You got your flashlight?" asked Jones, breaking the silence.

Vic reached into the pocket sewn in the interior lining of his coat and pulled out a small flashlight. He flicked it on and pointed it toward Jones, basking him in a bright white light. "Wasn't sure if this was the red one or not, kind of glad it isn't."

Jones didn't bother to respond but bent over and unzipped his duffel bag. After rummaging through it for a while, he pulled out his own flashlight and turned it on. Then reached back in and grabbed a couple towels, tossing one to Vic. They cleaned the mud off their shoes and pants as best they could and put the dirty towels in a plastic bag and back into Jones' duffel bag.

Jones zipped his bag and picked it up. "Follow me," he said as he began heading toward the basement stairs. "I figured instead of having you keep watch outside, you can watch through the hole I drilled in the front window while I setup the equipment."

"What's the matter, afraid to be in here by yourself?" asked Vic ruthlessly.

Jones didn't bother to respond, but started quickly climbing the creaky basement stairs, lugging his bag over his shoulder. Once they reached the first floor, they shined their flashlights around. Nothing seemed to have changed since they were here last. Vic continued to follow Jones down the hallway and up the stairs to the second floor. They made a U-turn at the top and headed down the upstairs hallway to the bedroom at the front of the house. When they reached the window Jones felt around the plywood boarding that covered the window until his fingers pressed into a soft spot and he scooped out putty that concealed the hole. Jones was right, when the black putty was in there it looked like a normal knot in the wood. Vic wouldn't have been able to tell it was there, even as close as he was.

"Keep an eye out, I'll be quick," instructed Jones, then he headed back out the room.

The hole was slightly below eye level so Vic hunched down a bit and peeked through, getting a decent view of the area in front of the house. Light from the moon illuminated the yard below and he spotted a flock of geese flying overhead in the distance. The slightest of breezes seemed to be blowing, swaying an old willow tree near the street and causing a sliver of bitterly cold air to brush against his face around his eye. After scanning the area Vic didn't see any cause for concern. It seemed pretty dead out there.

Vic patiently watched through the hole for what was

probably only a few minutes but seemed to take a good deal longer before Jones finally came back into the room carrying a small cylindrical camera with a wire dangling from it which ran all the way back out the door.

"Last one and we're good," said Jones as he walked up to the opening. "The laptop's booting up now."

Vic nodded and stepped back from the window, letting Jones work. It wasn't all that difficult, Vic found. Jones applied a clip that fit around the camera which secured the camera to the plywood. Then he applied putty to fill in any gaps that were left when the camera was in, and it was set. Then, without a word to Vic, Jones headed back out the door. Vic followed as they headed back to the master bedroom. The hardwood flooring creaked under their weight as they walked. Entering the bedroom, Vic saw the laptop was on a login screen as it rested on the floor. Jones bent over and entered the password and Vic got an unwelcome view of Jones' ass crack.

"Alright, let me just load this program and we should be good," said Jones as he waited for the computer to initialize.

"Take your time," replied Vic as he looked away, scanning the bedroom around him. His gaze rested on the familiar blood stain that he remembered from the last time they were here. A tingle of excitement fluttered through Vic as he realized he was looking forward to something similar happening again. A thought suddenly occurred to him. "Jones, you have those voice recorders, right?"

"Yeah, they should be in my bag. Help yourself," replied Jones without looking up from the computer. Vic bent over and searched through Jones' duffel bag, amazed by all the things he saw in there: power tools, flashlights, batteries, a mallet, crowbar, cables, snacks, water, and a first aid kit among some other bulky things tucked away further in. Vic rummaged through all that until he found two handheld devices with speakers on them.

"Alright, we're good." Jones called out. Vic looked over and watched the laptop screen with the four cameras. From what he could see it looked clear outside. He got up with the recorders and walked over to Jones.

"Before we go any further let's go over these things," said Vic, handing one of the recorders to Jones. "As soon as any weird shit starts happening I want you to bring this out and start using it, okay?"

"Yeah, I follow. What do we do though, just hit record and hold it out?" asked Jones.

"Actually, we should set these up first, the mic needs to be set to the highest sensitivity without any filters or noise cancelling options affecting the sound," replied Vic as he looked down at his recorder. He turned it on and after a while figured out how to adjust the mic sensitivity through the menu. Jones gave him his recorder and Vic did the same for other one.

"Okay, once we start experiencing anything unexplained, turn this thing on. If you start hearing footsteps or feel a cold spot in an area that seems electrically charged then stay in that spot and start asking questions. Who are you? Why are you here? Can you help us find the diamonds? Better yet, where are the fucking diamonds? Keep recording for as long as the activity is happening, even maybe five minutes after it stops."

"Got it," said Jones, looking at the recorder. "Then what, just play it back?"

"Yeah, and listen closely. If we picked anything up you should be able to hear it on the playback and if our paranormal friend is who we think it is, we might just get the location of those diamonds."

"Well, what are we waiting for?" Jones walked over to the blood stain and hit a button on his recorder. A red light lit up and started flashing. "I know you're here," Jones called out. "We're friends with Dean, he said you were a good friend of his. We need your help buddy. Tell us where you stashed the diamonds, just talk into this recorder in my hand."

Vic stood still and listened with anticipation, his flashlight illuminated Jones with the recorder in hand, casting a dark shadow against the wall. The ceiling let out a quick creak above them and they both looked up, uncertain if that was normal or paranormal. They waited this way for a while but only silence followed. It didn't seem like anything was happening just yet.

"Play that back, we probably didn't catch anything but just want to make sure," said Vic. Jones looked toward the recorder and after stopping it from recording, figured out how to make it play back. They listened as Jones' voice repeated his questions from earlier then Vic attuned his ears to pick up any small details in the recording that followed. He made out the creak from the ceiling and a bunch of static but no other sounds came through.

"Worth a shot," said Jones, sounding glum.

"Yeah, we got all night though. Let's keep at it. You notice anything strange then do what you just did and hopefully we can catch something," replied Vic.

"Alright, I think we covered a lot of the second floor last time we were here, why don't we check out the first floor?" Jones said as he walked over to his duffel bag on the floor and rummaged through it a while before pulling out a large rubber glove that he put on. "I'll even check the bathroom this time."

"Ha, thank you!" replied Vic, relieved. "I'll check around in the kitchen." He followed Jones down the stairs and down the hallway with flashlight's lighting the way. Jones went into the bathroom and Vic walked further to where the oak hardwood flooring ended and changed to the yellowish ceramic tile of the kitchen. Vic assumed the tile must have been white at some point but as he walked in and flashed the light on the ground, the tiles had a yellow tint to them and the grout had worn away leaving gaps between many of the tiles. He had the sudden thought to check the gaps between the tiles as maybe Marcus was bold enough to leave the diamonds in plain sight and spent the next few minutes with his flashlight on the ground walking along the lines of tile. He wasn't having any luck when Jones walked in and pulled off his rubber glove.

"I checked both holes of the toilet like you did upstairs and didn't find anything," said Jones, disappointed. "You checking the floor?"

"I thought Marcus might have been crazy enough to leave them in plain sight between the tiles thinking it was only a temporary spot." Vic shrugged, realizing he wasn't being very creative in his search.

"We need to think this through," said Jones, brow creased and hand on his chin. "Let's try and put ourselves in Marcus' shoes. You just got away with two of the rarest diamonds on the planet. You're shot in the stomach, movement is hindered, and you're in a lot of pain. After about a forty-five minute drive you finally make it to this house, for whatever reason he chose this place, and you get here. What do you do?"

Vic though about it, trying to imagine what Marcus would have done when he got here. He did his best to put himself in the mind of a hunter. Part of being a hunter is knowing your prey. They needed to get inside Marcus' head and figure out why he did what he did. "Well, the windows and doors weren't boarded at that point, I read in one of the newspaper articles that authorities first noticed his car parked behind the willow tree out front. They believed that he just came in through the front door by picking the lock." Vic nodded toward the boarded up door in the entryway. "So he gets in through the front door and then what?"

Jones thought about it for a while, then started heading back to the entryway. "Well, again he's injured so he probably didn't have the strength to lift anything heavy or climb anywhere, like in the attic." Jones put his hand under his chin in thought. "I don't know, let's look around for a minute. See if anything sticks out as a potential hiding spot that you'd consider using."

Vic nodded and followed Jones. They pointed their flashlights along the cracked walls and recessed floorboards as they walked down the hallway. The air was pungent and seemed thicker with mold than last time which made Vic feel like he wasn't pulling in a full breath of air. His head was beginning to ache. Maybe the strong winds actually helped ventilate the house and wondered if it would be better if the wind picked up.

When they got to the front door they turned around, inspecting the house before them. Vic was on the left and illuminated the living room with his flashlight, resting on the spot where Marcus had died.

"The biggest blood stain is right there," said Vic. "Maybe he didn't even get all that far and found some place around there to hide them."

"Then how did those stains get upstairs?" asked Jones.

Vic forgot about that. "Okay, so he got in, went upstairs, possibly hid the diamonds up there then came back down, sat up against the wall, and waited for them to show up? He knew they were able to track the diamonds, right?"

Jones' eyebrows raised at the question. "Yeah, he knew. Dean told him before the job. It's possible. How many stains were up there, just the two? Maybe he left them as clues?"

"Yeah, or maybe he left them to throw people off the trail. Were those the only stains you saw, the ones in each of the bedrooms? Maybe we should look around for more and see if we can retrace his steps?"

Jones shrugged and panned his flashlight around on the floor in front of them. The old oak hardwood was overly worn in this area and nicks and scratches were scattered about most of the boards. Vic added his light to the area and noticed a couple small dark circles that looked like they might be blood stains a couple feet in front of them. He nodded toward the stains, Jones looked down where Vic was indicating.

"You know, this might be from the other guy that died. He walked in and then bam, took a bullet," said Jones.

Vic looked back to the living room then to the stain. "So we got blood here that may or may not be his, blood in the living room, and in the bedrooms upstairs." A thought suddenly occurred to Vic. "We know Marcus ended up against the wall there, instead of retracing his steps from where he went when he came in the house, let's see if we can follow back from his last spot. He had to..."

Jones was about to interject when they both heard a faint buzzing noise coming from the bedroom upstairs. Jones' eyebrows shot up in alarm. "That's the motion sensor, something outside must have triggered it!"

Jones rushed up the steps and into the bedroom, Vic followed close behind. When they came into the room, Vic saw movement on the camera in the bottom corner of the screen. Three people were walking up to the west side of the house. As they drew near, Vic noticed they appeared to be teens, it looked like one guy and two girls. They carried bags with them which indicated they were likely intending to stay a while. They passed by the apple tree and moved to the back of the house under the view of the camera. Jones looked at him, eyes grave.

Of course it was too much to ask that things go through without a hitch. No job ever goes smoothly, something always goes wrong.

CHAPTER 9

The Other Side

The air was cold and brisk as they walked along the gravel road beneath the clear night sky. Crystal could see the house in the distance, illuminated by the full moon. It was just down the street from her house, not even two miles. What were the odds? The only land between them was the Henderson's farm, which they were coming up to on the right. The Henderson's were an older couple and kept to themselves and she didn't think they would mind if they knew her and her friends were sneaking into the old Smith home. Still, they did keep quiet as they passed and tried to avoid the perimeter of the street light outside their farm. Best to not attract any attention.

As they drew near, Crystal did her best to calm herself down. She had been looking forward to tonight for a while now. There was something about being in the house that was truly exciting and made her feel alive. She attributed it to the fact that not only were they trespassing, they were trespassing in a place where two people had died recently.

It was surreal to think about what happened there, at a place so close to her home. This was a town where nothing eventful ever took place but what transpired in that house made local headlines. The town couldn't stop talking about it.

Crystal remembered the first time they broke in and ascended the basement stairs. Her heart pounded in her chest as she made her way through the dark house. It was quiet, the air smelled musty and every one of her senses were peaked. She never felt anything like that before, it was a total rush! Since then, it's been the only thing on her mind. Her thoughts wandered to the house during class, while doing homework, and even in her dreams. It felt good to finally be going back. The fact that her best friends had joined her only seemed to intensify her excitement. She barely noticed how cold it was.

"Helloooo... Crystal," said Frankly softly, waving a hand in front of her face. Crystal realized she had been talking to her and was looking for a reply but she was too lost in thought to notice.

"Sorry, what? I was drifting there a bit," replied Crystal.

"No shit! I was asking what you wanted to do when we get there birthday girl."

"We can chill for a bit, get a feel for the energy of the place" Crystal finally said after giving it some thought. "Smoke a bowl."

"Sounds good to me," Ryan stated happily.

Crystal pulled her phone from her pocket and checked the time, swiping away notifications that had popped up on her screen. She wanted to focus and clear her head of any distractions, nothing else mattered tonight.

"Man that place looks creepy," muttered Ryan, looking at the house in the distance.

Crystal looked ahead, silently agreeing that it did look creepy from their position. The porch with the overhang that didn't connect to anything along with the weathered gray siding and boarded up windows gave her trepidation.

"What did you expect?" asked Frankie. "The place had been abandoned for—how long was it?"

"Four years," replied Crystal. "The previous owners had

grown old and stopped taking care of the place about ten years before that anyway. Then they finally lost the house along with their savings when the market crashed. They couldn't afford the property taxes on the land and weren't able to sell in time. A bank now owns the house and the land around the house. The Hendersons bought the farm land up to the barn there. The Coleston's bought the land on the other side."

Ryan looked thoughtful as he starred at the house. "Why didn't the bank just tear it down? And what happened to the back porch?"

Crystal giggled, "The Smiths were about to replace the porch when the market crashed and they lost their retirement savings due to a bad financial advisor. I was kind of sad to hear of their situation, they always mentioned that the house and property had important historical value and were deeply attached to it but ever since they became estranged from their son they got more reclusive so I never learned more. Sadly, I heard they both passed away shortly after losing the farm." She was genuinely sorry for them, they were always kind to her the few times she had met them. "As for tearing it down, the bank intends to from what I heard, but they need to do the same with the old barn back there. There's some old equipment in the barn and it sounds like it would be quite an expense to clear everything out and demolish both. Besides, from what I understand banks operate slowly. Who knows when they'll finally fork over the money for it." Crystal's gaze followed Ryan's as he eyed the barn.

"That thing looks worse off than the house, one strong wind could knock that thing over."

"I played hide and seek in that barn when I was younger," said Crystal, thoughtfully. "That thing is sturdier than you might think."

They approached the wooden fence that separated the farmland from the house's surrounding lawn and hopped over, coming to a halt under an apple tree. Crystal surveyed the land keeping an eye out for skunks which had been a problem around here lately, she saw one last time there were here and think it may have nested under the front porch of the house. Not seeing any small white-striped shadows scurrying about, they continued to the back of the house. A familiar tingle began to well up from the bottom of Crystal's stomach as they approached the loose boarding that led into the basement. The time had finally come!

"Allow me," offered Frankie, reaching down to pull the boarding loose. She knew how to slide it off and the boarding came off easily and was placed along the foundation wall next to the opening. Then she looked back to Crystal and held out her arm. "Birthday girl first."

Crystal smiled as she walked over and eased herself into the pitch black basement. Frankie and Ryan followed close behind.

* * *

Vic watched the screen intently with Jones by his side. They heard the board pry loose below, there was no denying it now. They had discussed this as a possibility but this was one of the situations Vic had been hoping deep down wouldn't happen. It was silly to keep that hope, he realized. In their line of work something's always bound to go wrong, it's just a matter of when.

Jones turned around and crept towards the door, doing his best not to let the floorboards creak. Vic followed, light and slow, trying not to make a sound. Jones slipped through the doorway and into the hall, leaving Vic surprised at just how nimble he could be when needed. Vic knelt down inside the doorway of the master bedroom, remaining still and silent.

* * *

Aside from the area just inside the window where a small sliver of moonlight shone through, Crystal was surrounded by darkness. It pressed close around her and she felt the uncanny sensation that someone, or something, was standing behind her in the dark. She always had that feeling when in the house though, that was one of the things that added to the excitement and she did her best to suppress that sensation, though she took a quick peak behind her. Frankie quickly made it through the window. Ryan took a little more time, not used to how far the floor was from the window but he slipped through and landed on his feet. Crystal pulled a lighter out from her pocket and flicked it on.

"So who brought the flashlight?" she asked, the flame from the lighter casting small shadows around her and the surrounding area.

"You said you were bringing everything!" exclaimed Frankie.

Crystal switched the flashlight on with her other hand, shining the light in her face. "Gotcha sucka."

"Nice," replied Frankie, not laughing. She walked back to the window and reached out and slid the plywood boarding back in place over the window. They were securely in now.

Crystal panned the light around the room, noticing some footprints on the floor from dried mud that she didn't recall seeing last time. It wasn't hard to imagine that other people had the same idea and wanted to check out the house. She was sure she could ask around school and find out who it was. Other than that, not much had changed. The air still felt cold and musty, and creaking noises could be heard overhead. Ryan was looking up at the ceiling, noticing those sounds as well.

"The house creaks and shifts with the wind, you'll get

used to that," Crystal said to him. She lowered her voice and added a tone of mystery, "Though some of the noises could be the ghosts. We should head up there to find out."

"Right," replied replied, still looking up.

Crystal made her way to the bottom of the staircase on their left. Once at the bottom, she scanned up the stairs with the flashlight. The door on the first floor landing that led into the hallway was open and she was sure they closed it as they were leaving last time which again confirmed that someone else had been in here looking around. She started ascending the staircase with Frankie and Ryan following close behind.

"Let me know if you sense anything as we check out the house," whispered Crystal as she slowly climbed the stairs, making sure her feet were firm on the wobbly boards.

"If I scream, you'll know I sensed something," Ryan joked.

Crystal chuckled. The excitement she felt upon entering intensified as they made their way up the stairs but Ryan's levity helped lighten the mood. She was glad he came.

Once she reached the top of the stairs, she turned left and used the light from the flashlight to inspect the first floor hallway. She noticed some more footprints on the hardwood floor, but after scanning from the kitchen to the entryway it didn't look like anyone was here at the moment. The house was dark and quiet. Her heart began beating faster as she walked through the doorframe into the hall, she could feel it in her chest. Frankie and Ryan remained close behind her.

"You're right, this place has a certain feeling," said Ryan quietly, looking around. "Maybe it's just me."

"No," whispered Crystal, "I feel it too. That's why I've been wanting to come back here so badly."

She looked left toward the entryway to the house, the room to the right of that door is where she saw what had to be blood stains from the homicide. They would be spending most of their time in that room but for now she turned back around and headed toward the kitchen. There was a short countertop on the far wall that separated the kitchen from the dining room and Crystal placed the flashlight on its dusty surface then reached into her purse and pulled out a small circular candle with a tin base. It wouldn't be wise to keep using the flashlight all night or the battery could die. She lit the candle then turned the flashlight off.

"So far, so good," said Crystal as she glanced around the room, her gaze resting on Ryan at the end. "Now seems like a good time to pack that bowl."

Ryan had been looking around the house with an uncertain expression but reached into his pocket and pulled out the baggy. "Past time as far as I'm concerned. I need something to help right me up. This place is creeping me out." He opened the baggy and took out a fat bud covered with white crystals and orange hairs. Ryan reached in his pants pocket with his other hand and took out a glass bowl.

While Ryan broke up the bud and packed the bowl, Crystal took out her smartphone and placed it on the counter, deciding to get some music going to help liven the place up and ease the tension further. After picking one of her favorite playlists she turned up the volume on her phone then raised her arms and started dancing to the techno-trance beat that played through.

Ryan finished packing the bowl and handed it to Crystal, who still had her lighter in hand and sparked it, taking a long, deep hit. While holding it she passed the bowl to Frankie who took a hit then passed it to Ryan. She was just going to do one to get the ball rolling, it was going to be a long night anyway so no sense in getting too fucked up too soon.

"Ah, much better," stated Ryan as he exhaled, obviously mellower. "I was getting antsy there."

"I could tell," replied Crystal, still swaying with the music. They chilled to the music for a while letting the weed take the necessary time for its effects to be felt. Odd sounds could still be heard coming from the house. Ryan kept looking around anxiously, she could tell he was a little nervous and the weed probably didn't seem to be helping with that just yet. She was anxious too but it was more from excitement, she wasn't really nervous.

A sudden knocking noise came from down the hall and was well heard over the music, startling the group. Crystal immediately recognized this wasn't a typical creaking sound the house usually made. They all looked down the hallway, remaining quiet and attentive. The candle illuminated the kitchen and dining room area and only slightly down the hallway to the basement door, it was dark beyond that.

Crystal paused the song on her phone then grabbed the flashlight off the counter and flicked it on, shining light down the hallway. A bright circle lit up the boarded up entryway door, they didn't see anything obvious that could have caused the noise. She began moving toward where the sound had come from, at least where she thought it came from, it was hard to tell exactly. The hardwood flooring creaked with every step and once they reached the middle of the hallway she held up her hand, everyone stopped.

Crystal listened.

It was eerily silent for a change. She moved the flashlight around, seeing only the usual faded wallpaper, dirty flooring, and peeling paint from the ceiling. There were definitely new tracks all around the floor but it was hard to tell how recent they were. The room with the blood stain was coming up on the right and she pointed her light toward the archway, moving forward in that direction.

"Do you see anything?" asked Ryan softly from behind, nervousness in his voice.

"Nothing unusual."

They crept forward, huddled as a group, passing through the archway and into the living room where the homicides had taken place. On the floor, underneath a boarded up window, she saw the oval shaped stain that she knew had to be blood. A shiver overcame her as she approached, her muscles tensed.

"What is that?" whispered Ryan.

"I'm pretty sure that's where one of the men died," replied Crystal with a genuine sadness in her voice. "We should leave the offering there."

Frankie nodded in agreement. They stood in place for a moment but nothing else caught their attention. It was cold and the occasional creak was heard but nothing unexplained happened further.

"Alright, let's grab the Ouija board and stuff, and move back over here. I just have a feeling that something might be trying to come through," said Crystal after a while. They walked back to the kitchen and each grabbed some things to bring over. Crystal grabbed the Ouija board and planchette out of her backpack, Ryan grabbed the bottle of moonshine and some cups, and Frankie grabbed the bowl and an extra candle. They made their way back to the living room and began setting up. Crystal placed the Ouija board on the ground with the wooden planchette on top as Frankie lit the candle and placed it near the board. Once everything was setup she motioned for Ryan to hand her the bottle and cups.

"Here you go," said Ryan as he handed the items over. "Pour me a cup, I'll take mine straight."

Crystal nodded and set four cups on the floor, pouring a small amount of the clear alcohol into each cup, then handing one to Frankie and Ryan. The forth she placed on the blood stain then spoke aloud. "We offer this to you in hopes of communicating with anyone who may be here from the other side. We mean you no harm and just want to speak with whoever still resides here. We know you are here. Please do what you can to communicate with us."

Crystal grabbed her cup off the floor and raised it up in toast, Frankie and Ryan bumped theirs to hers.

"Happy Birthday," Frankie and Ryan said in unison as the cups clinked then each took a sip.

Crystal coughed as the liquid burned a path down her throat. "Jeez, how much alcohol is in this?"

"It's like a hundred-and-sixty proof, eighty percent alcohol," replied Ryan while doing a better job of getting his down. "It's all I could get. I told you to bring some juice to mix it with."

Crystal shook her head, it felt like she was breathing fire but the burning subsided and she did her best to just breathe. After a few seconds the pain passed and she placed the cup back on the floor. "That stuff is horrible!"

Frankie and Ryan just chuckled, Crystal noticed Frankie seemed to be feeling the same and watched her place her unfinished cup down as well.

"Why don't we try using this thing," said Ryan, placing his hand on the planchette.

"Alright," Crystal began, "let's settle down. We need to focus our intent and open ourselves up to the spirit world. She took a deep breath then placed her hand on the planchette next to Ryan's. Frankie placed her hand on it as well. They sat in silence for a while, each slowing their breathing and calming their mind.

Crystal closed her eyes. "Who's here in this house with us?" she asked aloud, keeping her eyes shut. "Please tell us your name."

A sudden thump sounded from the room above them, startling the group. A spike of fear shot through Crystal at the sound and they each pulled away from planchette on the Ouija board. Crystal grabbed the flashlight off the floor and turned it on, pointing it up towards the ceiling.

"What the fuck was that?" asked Ryan in wonderment, looking up.

Crystal smiled, was that a direct response to their request for communication? With a very piqued curiosity, she did her best to gather up her courage. "Only one way to find out."

She got up off the floor and shone the light toward the staircase, its hand-rail and steps running up past the ceiling, and began walking towards it.

"Maybe we should have brought some protection or something," whispered Frankie.

"What do you mean protection?" asked Crystal as she looked back curiously.

"I mean a knife or gun, or something. What if someone really is up there? Maybe like, some bum is living up there or something."

Crystal thought about it a second but shrugged it off. There was no one here last time they entered and it's not like there's a problem with homeless people in their town. She didn't think it'd be likely one would found have found out how to sneak into this place. Besides they watched the house for a good twenty minutes as they approached. There was no sign of anyone around, or any activity in the house.

"Last time we were here we heard noises like that and there was no one upstairs. I think this place is haunted. I think something paranormal is causing the noises, and I want to go check it out," Crystal said firmly. Resolute, she started walking toward the staircase. She actually felt less nervous now, a courage seemed to have taken over. She reached the bottom of the staircase and pointed her flashlight over the top steps, not seeing anything on the upper landing.

"Alright ghosts," she called out, "I'm coming for you!" She began ascending the stairs, taking each step slowly and panning the flashlight back and forth as she climbed. Aside from the creaking boards under her feet the house was silent, eerily silent. She reached the upper landing, her heart pounding in her chest. Maybe it was the weed and the strong alcohol, but this felt way more exciting than the last time she was here. So far this night was working out perfectly.

Within the blink of an eye, her excitement turned to horror as a man rushed through the bedroom door ahead of her, placing a hand over her mouth before she could scream. She dropped the flashlight but before she did she saw what he held in his other hand. It was unmistakable and had a cylindrical attachment at the end which she knew was a silencer. Another man rushed out from the hallway to her left and flew down the stairs.

"You should have listened to your friend," the man holding her said, feeling the cold metal tip of a gun pressed against her forehead.

"Fuck with me and you are all history!" Crystal heard a man exclaim angrily downstairs. Whatever was left of the courage she had mustered melted away quickly and Crystal Diaz started to shake uncontrollably with fear in the man's grasp.

CHAPTER 10

Cold

Vic held on to the girl tightly from behind, his left arm under hers with his hand securely covering her mouth. The other hand held a piece of cold metal to her forehead. She was thin and almost a foot shorter than he was so he didn't have to struggle to keep her in check though he felt her tremble and heard a muzzled sob coming from under his hand. *She's just a girl,* Vic thought, not feeling good about pressing a gun against her head.

Jones had rushed down after her two friends and heard him pistol-whip one of them. The other surrendered easily after that and kept yelling not to hurt her. After what seemed like no time at all, Jones had his gun pointed at the head of a young man with another girl climbing the stairs in front of them, both with their hands in the air.

Vic waited and held on to the girl, deciding to let Jones take the lead. The young girl walking up the stairs in front of Jones had purple hair with blond roots and light skin with a stocky build. She looked at the girl in Vic's arms with concern and fear as she reached the top of the stairs. Jones held on to the other one with a gun pressed against the back of his head, he was skinny and had short dark hair with a bit of fuzz on his chin. Blood ran down from a gash on his forehead.

"Y'all picked the wrong day to fuck around in this house," said Jones gravely from the top of the stairs, the severity of his statement accentuated by the grimace on his face and intense look in his eyes. Jones held on tight to the teen's left shoulder with his other hand holding the pistol to the back of the guy's head though Vic noticed Jones was staring intently at the girl he held.

"You," said Jones, suddenly shifting his gaze to the other girl between him and Vic. "Head through that doorway into the room. Anyone tries anything stupid and I'll paint the walls with this kid's brain." The girl he motioned to trembled but managed to put one foot in front of the other and walked into the room. Vic nudged the girl he held forward, releasing his hand from her mouth though he held on to her left should and still held the gun to her head. Jones followed behind with the other one.

The master bedroom was mostly dark, they had closed the laptop when the teens had entered the house and the only source of light came in through the doorway from the flashlight that had fallen to the ground.

"Now, stand against the wall with your hands in the air," instructed Jones, leaving no room for argument.

Vic released the girl and the three quickly obeyed and stood against the wall by the door with their hands in the air. With his free hand, Vic grabbed the other pistol from his holster and turned off the safety, now pointing both guns at the two closest to him, the one he captured and the one Jones pistol-whipped. Jones lowered his gun then walked out the door and grabbed the flashlight off the floor from the hallway and came back pointing the light in their faces.

"You don't have any weapons or anything on you now, right?" asked Jones as he began patting down the one with purple hair. They shook their heads fearfully but remained quiet. Jones took his time patting them down and seemed to be extra thorough with the girl he had captured. Vic got the impression Jones was feeling her up and she cringed as he searched her. Jones had a sick smile on his face and Vic couldn't help but feel sorry for the girl as he watched Jones continue to grope her body.

"It's a damn shame you all had to come here tonight," Jones said softly. He finished his search and took a step back. "You can put your arms down." The three glanced at each other and slowly lowered their arms.

"What are you going to do with us?" the one with the gash on his cheek asked meekly.

Jones looked to Vic intently, "I think you know what we have to do." There wasn't any kindness in his voice.

Vic shifted in his stance, his guns still trained on the girl and the other one in the middle who began squirming after hearing what Jones said. Vic felt uneasy but did his best to appear calm and cool.

"No, you don't have to do that!" the kid in the middle shouted. "Please! We won't struggle. Do what you need to do here and we'll just... we'll do anything, just leave us alone. There's no reason to kill us!"

Vic hesitated.

Jones turned his attention to the one in the middle, "I don't like squealers." The kid continued to shake and sob but did his best to remain silent.

Vic knew what Jones was expecting him to do though he looked at Jones hoping for any indication there might be another way. Jones looked away from the kid and glanced back at Vic, face expressionless. Vic looked back at the two he had guns on, focusing on the kid in the middle. He couldn't bring himself to look the girl in the eyes. He stared down along the top of the gun in his right hand, panning it slightly to the left so it pointed directly at the kid's forehead. It was cold in the room and it was becoming an exertion to keep his arm steady but Vic felt his face flush as fear and uncertainty swept through him. He knew pulling the trigger would cross him over to a place he wasn't sure he wanted to be. An old memory flashed in his head and he couldn't help but hear his father's words in his mind.

"I'm afraid son," his father had said from a bed in a small room in the intensive care unit of the hospital. He was connected to an IV with tubes and wires running out from his arm into monitors that circled the bed. Vic had looked into his father's eyes and knew death was near.

Vic tried to be strong for him, he tried to comfort him in a way that he thought would make his father proud. After all, he wasn't a kid anymore. Vic had looked into his father's eyes trying to be strong and supportive. "You need to be fearless dad."

His father's face softened at the words though it was clear that he was still in discomfort and pain. Eyes watering, his father finally managed to respond with a soft strength in his voice. "When I told you to become fearless son, it was out of hope that you wouldn't let some trivial fear control you. That you would be brave when confronted with fear or uncertainty. I didn't mean for you to take it so much to heart. Most people are afraid. It's only natural. I'm afraid right now and I'm not ashamed." Tears rolled down his eyes and Vic's eyes watered as well.

"It's okay to be afraid. It's when you live completely without fear that you start heading down a dark road. You become cold, uncaring—reckless. You don't fear the repercussions of your own actions. You don't fear death! Now, I'm not saying you shouldn't take chances. You need to live your life. You need to love." His father grabbed his hand, his grip surprisingly strong. He looked intently into his eyes. "But I've seen you lately and I know what's going on behind those eyes. You pretend to not fear anything. You seem distant, cold. I don't want you going down a dark path. Promise me you won't."

Vic looked past the gun to young man trembling against the wall, knowing that once he pulled the trigger there would be no going back. He wouldn't hesitate the next time he had to take a life, he would be cold and it would get easier and easier each time after that. He made a promise to his father that he wouldn't go down that road, but if he didn't do this right now Jones would take it as a sign of weakness, or an unwillingness to do what needed to be done. Jones might even kill him over it.

The diamonds came back to mind and the job at hand. Vic knew something like this was bound to come up. Why was he struggling with it now? He promised his father but he also promised Dean to do whatever it took to finish this job. Vic knew what he had to do regardless of how much it bothered him. He narrowed his eyes and steadied his hand, focusing on the kid and drowning out everything around him.

Please forgive me father.

Jones started laughing which startled Vic and he relaxed the tension on the trigger. It was a deep, long laugh and when it was over Jones looked back over to Vic who could only stare back speechless. "Well, what are you waiting for? Grab some rope and tie them up!"

Vic still stood there, arms outstretched with guns trained, uncertain.

"What? Were you going to shoot them?" asked Jones, incredulously. He laughed again. "I'm sorry about that," said Jones, turning his attention to the teens on the floor who only looked back at them in fear and uncertainty. "My partner here is one cold-hearted son of a bitch. You're right though, there's no need to kill you. Of course, we can't let you go just yet."

Jones got right in the face of the one on the left who pressed back against the wall, still very fearful for her life. "You come here looking for adventure?" Jones shifted to the teen in the middle, "excitement?" He moved to the girl on the right, his face less than an inch from hers, "Well you got it."

Vic lowered his guns, still unclear as to what was going through Jones' head. Jones still stared at the girl who couldn't bring herself to meet his eyes and sobbed with tears streaming down her cheeks. After an uncomfortable length of time, he moved away and turned around, bending over to turn the laptop back on.

"What are you waiting for?" Jones asked Vic, losing the humor in his voice. "You three, sit down." The three looked at each other then sat down against the wall.

Vic grunted and shook his head, then went over to his duffel bag on the floor, looking for rope. He had to steady himself when he got on one knee to check his bag. A fraction of a second more and he would have shot that kid in the face. It was distressing how close he had gotten to crossing the line. This was not working out the way he thought it would. He had a feeling Jones was just delaying the inevitable and would still make him do this before the night was over.

"Anybody know you're here?" asked Jones as he crouched by the laptop. Vic looked over at the teens who looked at one another, uncertainly.

"No, we didn't tell anyone," one of them said nervously, the one in the middle with a gash on his forehead.

"Good," replied Jones, he actually appeared to be jovial again. "Now, how long were you planning on staying here tonight?" asked Jones as he entered the password to get back into his laptop. Vic found the coiled rope and brought it out of the bag.

"Most of the night," the same teen responded though his voice cracked as he replied between sobs.

"Why did you come here in the first place?"

"Just to hang out and ghost hunt, party a little."

Jones nodded his head, attentive, "I understand, trust me, I do. I've been in your shoes before. It's a creepy old house and you wanted to get a little fucked up, it's cool. So nobody's expecting you anytime soon, at least until morning?"

"Yeah, that's right."

"Perfect," Jones responded with a smile.

Vic got up with the rope, noticing that Jones had brought the cameras back up and there was nothing noticeable on screen, which was a relief. They were in the dark for a lot longer than he cared to be. Vic bent over and starting binding the hands of the girl on the left. Mascara stained tears ran down her cheeks from underneath dark bangs with blue tips. Her eyes looked up and met his.

"Why are you guys here?" the girl asked softly. She stopped trembling at least and Vic saw a certain bravery in her eyes. He respected that.

"What do you think?"

"I think it has something to do with the homicides that took place," she replied in a quiet reserved manner.

Vic looked over to Jones, who was staring blankly at the girl. He didn't appear to be jovial anymore. Vic turned his attention back to the knot he was making. "That's not your concern." Jones started rummaging around in his bag on the floor.

Vic was concerned over what Jones had in mind for these kids tonight. So far they had no clue where the diamonds were and it seemed like whenever they started making progress something interfered and kept them from moving further along with their search. They had nothing to go on that would help them narrow down the search area and there was no firm guarantee the diamonds were even in the house. Now with these kids here, they were severely pressed on time. Vic was starting to see the futility of what they were doing and couldn't help but feel agitated and disheartened.

Vic finished tying up the girl and used a pocket knife he kept in his jacket to cut the rope, then moved over and began tying up the one in the middle. Jones got up and cut a piece of rope to bind the other teen. They worked in silence, no one seemed to have anything further to say. Once they finished Vic looked to Jones. "Should we gag them?"

"Nah, I have an idea. I couldn't help but smell something very noticeable downstairs," said Jones. He got on one knee and started feeling around the pocket of the guy in the middle. "I know I felt something in that pocket," said Jones as he pulled out a baggy with a fat green nugget inside.

"Ah, good old weed," said Jones as he opened the bag and sniffed. "Mmm, that smells like some good shit." He looked to Vic. "Be a shame for them to stop partying on our account. What were you smoking this out of?"

"There's a bowl on the counter in the kitchen," the girl on the left said.

"Alright, thanks," replied Jones as he stood up looking toward the girl. "What was your name darling?"

The girl suddenly looked fearful and hesitated but finally replied, sounding uncertain. "Crystal."

Jones smiled, "Alright Crystal, I'll be right back." Jones walked out of the bedroom and down the stairs leaving Vic in the dark about what was going on. The three glanced at Vic who could only stare back and do his best to appear like he was in on Jones' plan. After an uncomfortably long absence, Jones was finally heard walking up the stairs and came back into the room.

"Still packed," stated Jones as he knelt down in front of Crystal. He brought the bowl to her lips and lit it. "Here, breathe deep." She looked uncertain, but took a hit. Jones let the bowl roast to encourage a bigger drag. Jones proceeded to do the same for the other two.

"Now, I know weed makes you thirsty so I brought some water as well," said Jones, flourishing a plastic bottle of water from his coat. He unscrewed the cap and bent over to bring it to the lips of closest one. He let each drink in turn, giving them a long swig.

"Good," said Jones, looking satisfied. "Now, I figured you might need a little buzz as it's going to get pretty boring from here on out. On your feet kid." He looked down to the one on the right with the purple hair and helped her to her feet. "We're going to separate you and put each of you in one of the bedrooms, alone. I don't want you talking to each other and planning anything foolish. You're going to stay where we put you and you're going to keep quiet, understood?"

They all nodded in agreement. Jones nudged the one standing forward and walked her down the hall to the bedroom on the right. When he came back he did the same to Crystal, bringing her to the second bedroom across the hall on the left.

After he returned he knelt down to talk to the last one with the gash on his forehead that was still bleeding.

"Now, I want you to watch this screen here. You see any activity going on outside the house you let us know, but don't shout too loud. Got it?"

He looked at the screen then nodded in agreement, "Yeah."

"Good," replied Jones, then he got even closer to the kids face. "And if I catch you snooping around in that bag over there, I'll cut your fingers off one by one."

The kid nodded and Vic genuinely knew he was scared shitless and wouldn't try anything. Satisfied, Jones got up and looked back through the hallway, speaking loudly, "Now I want the rest of you to be quiet. We got some searching to do. If I hear any of you making any noises, you'll regret it." Jones motioned Vic to follow him downstairs. Vic nodded, hoping to finally find out exactly what Jones was up to. He followed him down the stairs and to the kitchen, noticing a candle burning in the living room by the blood stain and a little disturbed to see they setup an Ouija board on the floor. A candle burned in the kitchen as well.

"What the fuck is wrong with you?" asked Vic once Jones turned around. "I almost shot that kid in the face."

Jones shrugged his shoulders, "I know, I wanted to see if you would do it." He was pacing around the room almost in a nervous fashion but he appeared cool. "Took your sweet time deciding."

Vic interrupted, defensively, "Look man I have no problem taking out people that are out to get us—cops, other professionals, cowboys who try to be heroes—but I'm a thief not a murderer. Those are just kids, probably still in high school."

Jones stopped and looked at him, narrowing his eyes. "Yeah, but those kids saw your face man, they saw mine too. They go to the police and that gives them a huge link to us. Do you have a file with any police department?"

"No."

"Well I do," Jones began angrily, "and I damn sure ain't gonna let all I worked for be in jeopardy because I felt bad for some kids that were snooping around where they don't fucking belong. We have an unfortunate situation we need to deal with."

Vic tried to come up with a response but Jones was making sense and he knew it. Still, there had to be a way to get through this without killing them. They continued to pace around the room, lost in thought. He still didn't see why Jones stopped him from shooting. "So why tie them up?"

"No sense in cutting their lives short just yet. Why not have a little fun with them?" said Jones, nonchalant.

"What do you mean have a little fun with them?" asked Vic.

Jones looked up at the ceiling, lowering his voice, "I put some liquid acid in their water. You know, LSD? Actually, I put a lot in that water bottle. They are going to be tripping very soon."

Vic couldn't believe what he was hearing, "Man we have a job to do and time is running out. Anything we do to those kids tonight is only worth it if we find those diamonds. We don't have time to be fucking around with them upstairs!" Vic was almost to the point of yelling but did his best to keep his voice down. He paced around now trying to control his thoughts and reign in his anger. "And what are you doing with LSD anyway?"

Jones walked up to him and grabbed him by the both sides of the face, squeezing almost painfully hard. "Relax, we got all night," said Jones then he roughly pushed Vic away, sending him hard against the kitchen wall. Jones turned away and began walking back down the hallway. Vic stood in disbelief for a second, fuming that Jones would treat that way. He pushed away from the wall and began walking after him but Jones quickly turned around and raised his gun, pointing it right between Vic's eyes. Vic froze and stared at Jones in shock.

"Don't piss me off Vic," said Jones. Any humor or kindness he once had was gone. "We were getting along so well. I'd hate to have to ruin it." Jones had a crazy look in his eyes that made Vic realize that after spending three days with him, he didn't have the slightest idea who he was dealing with.

Vic put his hands up. "Alright man, calm down."

Jones starred at him for a while longer, seeming to be struggling with something though after a while he lowered his gun. He paused a while before he spoke. "You're right, we don't get shit if we don't find those diamonds but I need to be sure you have my back. I agree that it's a sad, unfortunate situation for those kids, but in our line of work, sometimes we have to hurt the innocent. As a professional that's what you signed up for. As my partner I need to know that you won't hesitate when that moment comes in a life or death situation, cause up there you hesitated big time."

Vic knew it was true. This job required him to be ice cold in these situations. His life and Jones' were at stake. He had no doubts that Jones would do what was needed to save his life, he needed to be able to do the same to protect Jones. Vic made the decision upstairs and he was resolute now. "I won't hesitate next time. I promise."

Jones nodded and holstered his gun. "Listen, I don't want those kids up there to die any more than you do. Now you asked why I brought LSD with me on this job. Maybe there is a way to complete this *and* at the same time let those kids live to see another day. I had considered this a while back on another job where unexpected company could arrive, and from my own experimenting around when I was younger. I came up with an idea of drugging people to the point where they won't remember what happened. So that's why I brought it with. It was all I was able to get my hands on in time for this trip. I can't say if I gave them a lethal dose or not but I guarantee you that if they wake up tomorrow they sure as hell won't be able to remember what happened tonight. They won't remember me and they won't remember you. That's the best solutions I could come up with. You have a better idea?"

Vic shook his head, now appreciating Jones' point of

view.

"Good, now I need you to trust me. When I tell you to do something, you do it. No hesitating. We clear?"

"Yes, absolutely," replied Vic.

"Good, hold on a moment." Jones walked back into the living room where the Ouija board was setup and walked back holding the clear bottle the teens had brought. He undid the cap a took a swig then handed it to Vic. "Here, maybe this will help settle us down."

Vic looked at the bottle and nodded in agreement. Jones handed him the bottle and he took a sip and grimaced from the burn of the strong liquor. He capped the bottle and placed it on the counter next to some other things the teens had brought. It did help settle his nerves a bit though Jones continued to pace around the kitchen for a minute before speaking.

"Alright, now I want you to search the basement. Look for any place where the concrete may have been patched up, cracks on the floor, whatever. Also check the trusses, the spaces between the foundation and the flooring we're standing on, any place he could have stashed those diamonds. I'll look around on this floor. We need to speed up this search and find these things now!"

"Will do," replied Vic earnestly.

Jones nodded and turned around, heading into the entry-way. Vic turned to the basement door and opened it. An itch was felt on his upper chest and he scratched it realizing it was the amulet and rosary, which felt cold against his skin. With all the excitement going on he forgot how cold it was in the house and it seemed to be growing colder as the night wore on. As he crossed through the doorway to the landing that led to the basement, Vic couldn't help but shiver.

CHAPTER 11

Divided

V ic descended the basement stairs using the flashlight to guide him down the wobbly, creaky steps into the darkness below. He was immensely troubled by Jones' behavior and still unnerved at having a gun pointed at him, uncertain whether the trigger would be pulled. That didn't seem like the person he had gotten to know these last couple days, something had changed. Vic suddenly wondered if Jones remembered to bring his amulet. He didn't recall seeing it anywhere in the room before they left. Could that have anything to with how Jones was acting? Maybe that's just how he was—unpredictable. Jones seemed prepared for tonight and the amulet seemed to help both of them get some restful sleep so he had to have it on him.

The amulet brought to mind the call with Al who felt confident the dreams they experienced were caused by the diamonds which meant they had to be around here somewhere. The dreams he had this last week were more vivid and unlike any he had before. Vic felt so close yet so far away. This situation was unravelling but they needed to see this through.

I will finish what was started. I will come through for Dean.

Vic repeated this over in his head and began scanning the immediate area, not certain whether he actually believed it or not, repeating the words over and over until they became hollow without meaning. It was cold and dark, and this was becoming more and more like the last place on earth he wanted to be right now.

He pointed the flashlight towards the ceiling at saw a mass of cobwebs hanging between exposed rafters, deciding he would check the ceiling last and instead panned down and scanned the concrete floor and walls. Numerous muddy footprints were scattered across the floor, many more than the first night they were here. Still, as Vic looked around the open room he did see a lot of places the diamonds could be stashed, almost too many places. He was going to have to give this area a thorough inspection which was going to take some time.

First place to start is the floor and walls, Vic thought. That was the more exposed area. He started in the corner at the bottom of the staircase and started scanning the concrete foundation, looking for cracks, gaps, any sign of something being covered up, or any place that could hold two small diamonds. There was plenty of dirt and small debris scattered about and he saw normal cracks running along the foundation wall but didn't see any obvious area that would be a good hiding spot.

Jones could easily be heard upstairs, the openness of the basement a chamber that seemed to echo and enhance the creaking of the hardwood floor above. Footsteps, doors and cabinets opening and closing, even what sounded like Jones just shifting in his stance could be heard easily. Vic tried to dismiss those sounds as best he could.

As he scanned the basement walls, the research at the library came to mind and he entertained the notion of finding a secret room or area in the basement. Considering the house was built in 1913 there could be some cold-war era bomb shelter on the property. Vic suddenly wished he had thought of that at the library where he could have researched that notion further. Still, without seeing any potential hiding spots along the wall there wasn't much else to go on right now.

He turned the other corner and was already half way along the far wall opposite the staircase when something caught his eye on the wall, close to the floor. Vic bent down and brought the flashlight close to get a better look. Three small brown stripes ran side by side a couple inches long vertically on the wall. Vic pressed his fingers against it, it looked like it might have been somebody smearing blood with their fingers. Was this another clue left by Marcus?

Vic panned his light around the area of the mark, seeing if any other smears were present and stopping on a simple thin smear that looked to be about a foot long. It went completely vertical giving Vic the impression it was pointing up so he moved the light to follow where the smear pointed. The concrete foundation wall ended and it didn't look like anything was resting on top where the first floor trusses left a gap, but Vic decided to reach up and feel around. He searched the whole area not feeling anything but when he pulled his hand away his palm brushed against something thin on top of the foundation wall. Vic felt around again and slid out what appeared to be a post card.

THE GREATEST SHOW ON EARTH.

These words stuck out in the center of the flyer in the middle of a circle. Vic realized it was an old flyer for the Ringling Bros. and Barnum and Bailey Circus. There was a slight smudge over the name that appeared to have been dried blood, Vic was almost certain of that. Did Marcus place this here? What did this mean?

Vic was staring at the flyer trying to puzzle out if there was any connection between it and the diamonds when he noticed his breath started misting in the beam of his flashlight as he exhaled. That was odd. He was pretty sure it wasn't doing that before. Was it getting colder in here? It was definitely chilly and the basement was the coldest place in the house. While he was wearing heavy clothes and had gotten used to the chill, it did seem suddenly cooler than it was earlier.

A quick shiver shook him as he began to feel a tingling sensation on his exposed skin, like a charged rubber balloon was right next to it. The mist from his hot breath seemed to get thicker and an excitement surged through Vic as he realized it was happening again! He quickly reached into his pocket, searching for the digital voice recorder.

A sudden noise came from the corner of the basement, by the boarded up window they used to enter. It wasn't Jones or any creaking coming from the floorboards upstairs, it came from down here. He was certain. It sounded like a rock or something was thrown as he heard a distinct clink followed by a second and third fainter noise as if it hit the wall then came to a rest on the floor. He pulled the recorder out of his pocket and pointed his flashlight to the spot where the sound came from.

Vic slowly walked closer, seeing what looked like a few pebbles on the floor though he had noticed quite a few of those which he assumed came from the old foundation wall that had crumbled away in spots, leaving what looked like jagged scars on the foundation wall. How did one end up moving so forcibly though? That couldn't have been natural. Vic approached the spot where he heard the noise then looked down at the digital recorder in his hand and pressed the record button. The little red light began blinking. It was now or never.

"Who's there?" Vic called out, his breath still misting as he spoke. He looked around as he asked, listening intently. The flashlight gave off a good amount of light but the surrounding darkness of the basement seemed to press in on him.

"If this is Marcus I want you to know that I'm on your side man. I know Dean, he sent us here to finish the job, to help you out." Vic spoke slowly and firmly. "Help us out man. Help us finish this job. Where did you hide them?"

Vic paused, listening. It still felt ice cold and his body shook, partly from the cold, partly from the excitement he felt. Something was here with him, he could feel the energy around him. His thoughts centered on the Red Diamond Eyes, he closed his own eyes and pictured them in his mind, trying to drown out any other thought and focus solely on the diamonds.

"Where are the diamonds?" Vic called out, slightly louder this time but just as firmly, his eyes still closed. Only silence answered, an uncommonly long silence. He didn't hear the creaking of footsteps above, didn't hear the house shifting with the wind. Jones must have been occupied as well as he didn't hear him moving around upstairs. Vic opened his eyes, glancing at the recorder in hand, its red light steadily flashing. He shone the flashlight around the room. Nothing seemed different than before. It was still cold, he still felt that static charge around him.

"I need your help man. I feel you there, feel you with me. Say something, speak into the recorder in my hand. Dean said if any part of you is still here that you will help us. He believes in you. We believe in you."

Vic was still when all of a sudden the sensation left, feeling almost the slightest breeze drift past him towards the staircase. The static charge was gone and his breath stopped misting. A calm, serene feeling washed over him. In a way, he felt a slight exhaustion but at the same time felt a little cleaner, more pure, like after a workout or long run. He just stood there for a while in stillness and silence. It was almost euphoric. The tension and anxiety he felt not long ago was gone and Vic enjoyed a moment of peace.

It dawned on him after a while that the house remained unusually quiet. Jones hadn't moved around upstairs in some time. Vic looked down and turned off the voice recorder, feeling that if he was going to capture something he would have gotten it by now. He stood there, basking in the fuzzy, peaceful feeling that remained when a long, horrid scream from the upper level of the house broke the silence, shattering Vic's tranquility.

* * *

It's all in your head.

Crystal repeated this over and over until the words became meaningless and spun through her head like lottery numbers in a vacuum tube. It had started out well enough, the night she had planned. The moon was full. It was a gorgeous, though slightly frigid night. Shortly after entering the house her dreams for this night were shattered. The two men played games with the lives of her and her friends. It too much to bear. Once the large brutish man left her alone in the upstairs bedroom with her hands tied up she felt things might just be alright. They were just looking for something then they would go.

It's all in your head.

As the minutes crept by a tense sensation had begun spreading through her muscles, exciting her senses. She started to grind her teeth, unconscious of it at first but harder as time wore on. Her muscles began to feel tight and stressed, and her senses began to feel enhanced. A tingling sensation reverberated through her that gradually phased in and out. She had felt this before and was becoming more and more convinced the man had put something in the water she drank.

It's all in your head.

Patterns began to emerge from the darkness surrounding her, like fractal images shifting in and out of nothingness. They vibrated into a physical sensation that pulsed through her, eventually becoming more and more vivid and intense as patterns encompassed her and flowed around her. She began hearing noises.

It's all in your head.

The darkness began to talk to her. It whispered in her ear.

It was light enough that words were indiscernible. Sometimes it seemed like music was playing outside her room, or someone was speaking to her from the floor below. It came and went with sensations that weaved through her as if the patterns she saw, things she heard, and energy that flowed through her were all linked to one unseen force. She closed her eyes but the patterns remained.

It's all in your head.

Her thoughts scrambled. She would be thinking deeply about one subject only to find she couldn't remember what her last thought was. Where was she? How did she get here? Crystal lay on the floor anxious and jittery, unable to stay still and unable to focus as random thoughts kept swirling through her head. The tension in her muscles continued to become more and more uncomfortable, to the point of pain. She couldn't stop grinding her teeth. Her head moved back and forth without her realizing it. It was more than just weed that coursed through her. The man had put something in her water. She was certain.

It's all in your head.

As the sensations began to peak and her visuals became more intense, the door to her room slowly creaked open. Crystal almost didn't believe it was happening at first, that her hallucinations were becoming more vivid but then a man stepped through, illuminated by a faint glow coming from outside the doorway, his stocky outline unmistakable even though she struggled to remember who he was and why she was here. The door closed behind him. The darkness returned. A terrible fear coursed through her.

The visuals she saw became more intense. Vibrant colors seemed to shift and change. She heard noises, something wanted her to think they were footsteps but that's not how footsteps sound, is it? Amid the tension and pain in her muscles, fear coursed through her, a feeling more powerful and devastating than anything she experienced before. Her heart pounded in her chest and felt like it was about to explode. Every nerve in her body seemed alive and reverberating with the shifting patterns and energy waves that rolled through her nervous system. Crystal closed her eyes and started whining.

It's all in your head.

"Don't be afraid girl."

The words seemed emerge from the nothingness around her. She was almost unable to comprehend what was being said.

"We're just going to have a little fun."

A painfully bright light suddenly filled her vision, blinding her and causing pain in her eyes. A hand touched her arm, firmly but not painfully so. It began moving back and forth, caressing her.

"No," she managed to whimper, trying to turn away but she was already pressed against the wall.

It's all in your head.

"I didn't ask your permission."

The voice was deep and menacing. She couldn't recall anything more frightening. Hands grabbed her firmly, pushing her on her back. She opened her eyes and squinted to see a face pressed close to hers. She remembered that face. His cheeks seemed to be covered with maggots that wiggled around like a beard and his face itself looked soft and mushy, almost like a newly released bubble floating for the first time. But the eyes—they pierced through her clothes, her skin, and right to her very heart, and she saw exactly what they wanted.

Crystal screamed.

❈ ❈ ❈

Vic rushed up the basement stairs taking two at a time, not caring if the wobbly boards gave way underneath. He reached the top and peered in the hallway, scanning the first floor with his flashlight. Jones was nowhere to be seen. He heard a second scream from above. It was almost painful to hear, Vic had never heard that kind of fear before and knew immediately what Jones was up to. He quietly moved down the hall and looked up the stairs to the second level then began ascending, doing his best to not make any noise as he climbed. When he reached the top he paused, looking into master bedroom ahead. An emptiness washed over him as he looked inside. The screen from the laptop still illuminated the room. Lying on the floor in front of it was the body of the dark haired teen they left watching the screen. A pool of blood spread out from where his deformed head rest against the floor.

Jones, what did you do?

Vic leaned over, placing a hand on the kids shoulder and moving him around so he could see his face. Lifeless eyes stared back at his. Blood dripped from a gaping hole in his forehead, the other end of his skull was partly missing and chunks of it were on the floor, along with pieces of his brain. Vic felt hollow and empty.

Struggling noises came from the other room. The emptiness inside of Vic began to fill with something else—anger. Vic stood up and turned around. Another scream was heard, fainter this time, followed by a thump as if someone was being hit. The screams ceased after that. Anger grew inside him and began to boil. Anger with Jones. Anger with himself. This wasn't who he was. This wasn't what he wanted to be. It was senseless.

Vic walked out of the bedroom and flashed his light across the hall to the door on the right. It was open and he could make out a body lying still on the floor. Vic knew the same fate befell the girl in that room as the one in the master bedroom. Why would Jones do this? Why didn't he let them live like he said he would?

With his free hand, Vic reached for the gun in his holster, fingers wrapping around the cold hilt. He drew it out as he walked, eyes intent on the closed door on the left. Vic slowly approached with gun trained.

* * *

It's all in your head.

She tried to resist, to push back against the hands that held her down and groped her, against hands that were trying to lift her sweater up but he was strong and she was weak. She bit down on his hand and he yanked it away and quickly brought it back, striking her in the face. It barely stung, her body was numbed by whatever it was that coursed through her. She barely felt a thing. The fear was overwhelming, it overcame her and she closed her eyes and retreated back into her mind, detaching herself from the situation.

It's all in your head.

Patterns continued to swirl through the darkness of her mind, a purple grid seemed to close around her. There was a comfort there. She began to feel safe in the grid. Crystal felt her body lift off the floor to be spun around and dropped back down on her stomach. Her body felt far away from her now. Whatever this man did to her didn't matter. The hands molesting her reached around her waist under her sweater, tugging at the tight yoga pants that clung to her hips when suddenly, they stopped.

* * *

Vic reached out with the hand that held the flashlight and gave the door handle a turn and a slight push with his free fingers. His silenced Glock ready in the other hand. As the door slid open the light from Vic's flashlight began to fill the room and Vic saw Jones on the floor with his pants around his ankles. He turned around, startled. The girl lay on her stomach with her pants tugged slightly down. Vic felt some relief knowing he arrived just in time.

"What the fuck man," shouted Jones angrily, looking up from the end of Vic's pistol.

Vic remained silent and walked forward, gun still trained at Jones' head.

Jones seemed to ease up as Vic drew near and he put his arms up. "It's cool man, I'm just having a little fun with her." He gestured with his right hand to the girl on the floor as he spoke. "You can hit it when I'm done."

Vic looked at the girl, her arms were wrapped around her chest and head, and she was visibly shaking. Vic was still very angry but completely collected. "I'm not a rapist Jones."

Jones grunted, almost amused. He put his hands down by his sides. "Suit yourself. Just put the gun down and let me finish up here. Then I'll take care of her."

"I can't let you do that," replied Vic, softly but with an edge to his voice. "Besides, I thought you said we were going to let them go."

Jones cocked his head, not appearing to like his response and obviously angry, "I've been here almost two weeks now man! All cooped up in that stupid motel room! I'll I'm asking for is a little fun with this one to take care of the urges that make us men. Is that too much to ask?"

"She's too young Jones, and this isn't what I signed up for."

"So what are you going to do then, shoot me?" exclaimed Jones. "I saw how comfortable you are with that sort of thing in the other room. And what will you tell Dean?"

Vic remained silent. Jones leaned forward a bit while putting his left hand up. He spoke gently this time, "Don't cross me like this man. Put the gun down. We'll work this out." Jones gestured with his left hand to lower the gun. Vic didn't almost notice in time but Jones was doing something with his right hand and suddenly pulled his arm out brandishing a gun but Vic was quicker and unloaded four shots. The gun dropped from his hand and Jones gargled as he struggled to breath, eventually falling over.

"I didn't hesitate this time," Vic said softly.

* * *

It's all in your head.

She heard them talking back and forth, heatedly. The words echoed and shifted as they talked and were meaningless when they reached her ears. She did her best to keep her eyes shut and lay silent. Lost in whatever drug it was that coursed through her.

After what seemed like an eternity, a hand pressed against her shoulder gently shaking her. She heard what must have been words but they sounded like they were coming through water and bubbled away before she could understand what they meant. Another hand pressed against her and she cringed, though it seemed to be pulling her sweater down. She had been shaking uncontrollably and still was, she realized. A hand pressed against her forehead. Crystal looked up from the ground to see another face, mushy and shifting like the other but she sensed kindness from this one. It drew close and she leaned back. She saw lips moving and heard muffled words again, though louder this time, and she finally understood what was being said.

"You going to be alright."

CHAPTER 12

One Half of Me is Yours

Vic looked down at the girl with concern. She was sobbing and squirming about on the floor, muttering incoherently. Her pupils were dilated and she stared around blankly wherever she looked. She was pretty far gone. Vic had dealt with people on psychedelic drugs before and could tell.

How much LSD did Jones put in that water?

It didn't matter. It was done. Jones lay on his back close by. His pants were pulled down to his ankles and a pool of blood grew underneath him. A smelly pile of shit formed as well, it was a disgusting sight. Vic felt no remorse though, he did what he had to.

"It's in your head," the girl muttered almost indiscernibly. She sounded incredibly distraught. Vic looked back to her, he needed to get her out of this room. Hell, he needed to get out as well. The smell was making him nauseous.

"Alright my friend," said Vic gently as he bent down to help her up. "Time to get moving. How about we move this party downstairs?"

"No," she grunted as he took her arm and put it around his shoulders. She resisted, slightly, but didn't put up much of a fight. Vic grabbed on to her waist and pulled her up to her feet, struggling to keep the two of them upright. Once it seemed she was balanced and took a step forward she looked down and vomited on the floor in front of them, her body clenched with the heaves and she almost fell forward into the puddle though Vic managed to keep them both standing. He guided her around the puddle.

Ever so slowly, they made their way out of the bedroom and down the hall. Vic grimaced as he saw the stairs, worrying that he wouldn't be able to support her as they went down so he reached down with his free hand and scooped her up under the knees. Better to just carry her then have them both fall down the flight of stairs.

"It's alright, I got you," said Vic as she mumbled something he couldn't make out. Spit and vomit still ran down her chin and her mascara smeared eyes looked glossy and distant. Vic descended the steps slowly, making sure his footing was secure. The steps creaked and some shifted under the added weight of the two of them but he managed to get them both down to the landing and turn down the hallway to the kitchen. A small candle still burned on the counter providing some illumination. He gently set her down beneath the counter and reached into his pocket, grabbing a piece of clean cloth to wipe off her chin.

The girl muttered softly, moving her head back and forth. Vic shivered, wrapping his hands around his chest and under his armpits. It was bitterly cold and as the night wore on he could feel the cold bite harder though his jacket. He bent down and looked through the bag on the floor, the one the teens brought. It was full of snacks, bottled water, and something wrapped in cloth. He grabbed one of the bottles of water and unscrewed the cap then brought it to the girl's lips and encouraged her to take a sip. She resisted, but did end up drinking a bit then nudged the bottle away as he tried to give her more. Vic just put the cap back on and placed it in her hand, closing her fingers around it. When he released her hand the bottle just fell to the floor and Vic righted it and left it close in case she needed it. Vic rose and walked around in circles, the gravity of the situation sinking in.

"Holy shit, holy shit," he uttered as he walked. There were three dead bodies upstairs, he had a girl down here that probably needed medical attention, and it fell on him to finish the job and find the diamonds. The urge to give up overwhelmed him and he brought his hands to his head and rubbed his temples. He could go, he thought, run back out of the house, back through the winding creek that led to their hidden car, back to the motel and back to Chicago. He could call 911 from a payphone to report a situation at the house and leave, falling back into the arms of his girlfriend. Would she even talk to him if she knew that he was part of what happened here? Could he even tell her? Would he be able to go on as if nothing happened?

"They're here," the girl said. It was a simple phrase but it cut through his thoughts like an arrow. Vic recalled the walk in earlier tonight. It seemed so long ago. The constellations shone down from above, the distant stars seemed to guide their way. Orion would be out by now, Vic thought, as a stillness passed over him. He was a hunter, he was a man who got things done and it was on him to finish the job. Dean was depending on him. The two kids upstairs—the only way Vic thought he could get over this was by completing the job. After that he would go back to Shelly and try to forgive himself for what we was an accomplice of today.

Vic turned around and glanced at the girl on the floor. She seemed to be staring back at him blankly, almost as if she was looking through him. He turned around, not seeing anything behind him that would be the focus of her attention. When he turned back, he noticed her breath was misting as she exhaled and Vic saw that his was not. He leaned in close and put his hand on her shoulder. The air was ice cold around her and he noticed goosebumps along the exposed part of her skin but she didn't seem bothered by the cold.

"Outside," she said with her eyes staring straight ahead, unmoving, unblinking. Her pupils were dilated almost to the whites of her eyes.

"I'm here," she whispered, and immediately afterward her head fell forward and her body slumped to the floor. Vic was able to catch her before her head hit the floor and it seemed as if she passed out after that. Vic gently laid her down and put the bag under her head, propping it up a bit.

She seemed pretty still and Vic bent in close to make sure she was still breathing then got up and quickly rushed to the staircase and began running up the stairs. *Outside? I'm here? What does that mean? Was somebody outside? Did the Sheriff show up again?* Vic hastily reached the top of the stairs, distraught over having to see the young man's eyes still open and staring lifelessly at the wall. He reached down and respectfully closed his eyelids.

Jones' laptop was still on and Vic felt the slightest bit of relief at not seeing any activity outside the house. There were no cars along the street. No movement on screen. *What did she mean by outside?*

Vic walked back to the staircase and sat down on the top step, realizing he had been on his feet for a while and needed a moment to rest and gather his thoughts. He pressed his face into his palms and rubbed his temples. Did anything she say mean anything? Are the diamonds outside? Was it the ghost she was referring to when she said those things?

A sudden thought occurred to Vic just then, he reached into his pocket and took out the digital voice recorder, turning it over in his hand. He turned it on and played the recording from the basement, listening intently.

"Who's there?" he heard himself ask, turning up the volume as he played the audio recording back. There was a lot of static but he did his best to pick up the faintest sounds. He heard himself speak again, talking about his connection with Dean, then asking for Marcus' help. Static continued...

"Where are the diamonds?"

...Vic waited patiently when he thought he heard something. He rewound the recording a few seconds and played it back, bringing the speaker closer to his ear. Yes! He drew in a sharp breath as he heard it again, more clearly this time.

It can't be!

He rewound it again just to be certain it wasn't his mind playing tricks on him and played back the recording. A voice definitely could be heard that was not his own. It sounded like a man's voice but distant and soft, almost like a whisper.

"Barn," the voice said.

Outside, the barn!

Vic reached into his pocket and took out the flyer he had found in the basement before the recording. Of course, the smudge he saw was just under the first part of Barnum, under Barn! It was a clue! Excited, Vic stood up and rushed down the stairs, thrilled at the revelation he just heard. When he reached the bottom step the board shifted and Vic lost his balance. His ankle rolled and he came crashing down on the landing below, sliding on his stomach and dropping the voice recorder that slid along with him. Feeling foolish but largely uninjured, Vic stood up then bent over to pick up the recorder by his feet. That's when he noticed pieces of glass falling out the bottom of his fleece.

* * *

Sheriff Eli Hurth pulled his cruiser into the Main Street Inn parking lot then shifted the car into park. It was a brisk, clear evening and he was trying to follow up on a hunch from earlier. Leaving the engine running, he opened the door and stepped out, walking up to the main office. It was a slim chance he was taking but the night was calm and this was the last place to check. The dream from the other night kept bugging him and he hadn't been able to shake the belief that something bad was going to happen soon. Compelled to act on his instincts he felt the need to find out more about the two gentlemen he encountered the other day. He opened the door to the Main Street Inn and walked up to the counter.

"How's it going Earl? How are the wife and kids doing?" asked Eli, giving the clerk a quick nod as he approached. He had spoken with Earl many times in the past and considered him a friend. Emerald Ash was a small town and Eli had made it a point to get familiar with all the townsfolk. The man that sat behind the counter was elderly and balding, and had a distinct mole on the right side of his cheek. Eli also knew he walked with a limp, an injury he took while serving in Vietnam. He had served there too though in a different unit. They talked about the war many times.

"Dotty's fine. The oldest is in his first year of college over at NIU, he seems to be doing pretty well with his classes," replied Earl, curiously. "What brings you in?"

Eli shrugged. "I'm just looking into a couple of things. I ran into two gentlemen the other day over near the Smith property and was curious to see if they were still in town. I checked the other motels in the area and they didn't know of these two, but you're the last on my list to check. I'm looking for two men that go by David and Paul."

Earl's face lit up immediately when he heard the names. "Yes, I have two fellows by that name registered here. Paul Carpenter, a reclusive stout fellow, checked in almost two weeks ago. Keeps leaving the do not disturb sign up. The other one just got here three days ago I think. He checked into a separate room. He's also been leaving that sign on the door."

Eli's brow creased, he was intrigued as to why one of them had arrived almost two weeks ago if they were just helping a friend move. "What room are they in?"

Earl looked down to his register, running his finger along the list. "Paul is in room 113, and David is in room 117."

Eli nodded, "Appreciate the help Earl. You have a good

night."

"Everything okay with them Sheriff? Anything I should know about?" asked Earl as Eli turned to walk away, he was noticeably worried.

"I'm gonna pay them a visit. I'll let you know if there are any concerns," replied Eli. He left the office and walked down the sidewalk to the rooms, coming to a stop at room 113. He knocked and waited. The light was off and it seemed quiet inside. After knocking again Eli was sure that Paul either wasn't in or that he wasn't going to answer.

Looking to his right, he scanned the rooms and saw the door for 117, noting that the light was off and the room seemed dark as well. He approached and gave a knock, waiting for a couple seconds and listening for any activity inside. This room seemed empty as well so Eli turned around and headed back to his car.

Something wasn't adding up with their story. Why would one of the men arrive two weeks ago if he was helping a friend move? Why would they get rooms for this long? Seemed the friendly thing to do for the person who was moving would be to offer them a place to stay. Not satisfied with the conclusions he was making, Eli Hurth decided to patrol by the Smith house, unable to shake the suspicion that the two men were up to something.

He opened the door to his cruiser and hopped in. He backed out and quickly pulled out onto State Street heading west, flooring it.

* * *

Her fingerprints swirled and the creases in her palm swayed with the energy that flowed through her as she stared wondrously at her hands. Crystal had retreated to a deep corner of her mind while something else had taken over. Terrified, and disturbed by what was happening to her a little while ago, she allowed it to happen. Now she felt guided by some unseen force that she willingly surrendered to.

It was no longer unpleasant, that pain was behind her. It had gradually built and peaked until it finally broke through and became a thing of ecstasy. Now she plateaued, in a state almost detached from her body, purely part of the moment. The past was forgotten. She didn't know how she got here, didn't know where this place would lead her. It didn't matter. Only the present mattered and the feeling of oneness with herself, and with the house around her.

A candle flickered above her casting light and shadows that danced around the room, enthralling her with mesmerizing patterns that shifted in tune with the dancing shadows. Whispers could be heard, sounds that seemed to come from the farthest corners of the room, then speak as if right next to her ear in a benevolent voice, not frightening at all. It was bewitching.

"Look," she head a voice say.

It was a single spoken word yet she felt it burn into her like a tattoo and reverberate around her. She stared down into her hands again, this time noticing a deep crease along the center of both palms. The creases wriggled then slowly split apart, like the eyelids of a newborn baby, revealing a deep void beneath. She gazed far into the void, sensing a vastness inside as great as an ocean and as grand as the universe above and beyond.

In this vastness two red orbs emerged. They slowly approached, expanding as they drew near, each orb swirling with a million shades of the deepest red she ever saw. They pressed against the inside of her palms, a dark sliver began forming in the core of each orb, like a mist, and an understanding flooded her mind. Deep red eyes stared back at her from her palms and she gazed long into the darkness at their core. After a while, unable to properly gauge the passage of time in her condition, her skin slowly closed back over the orbs, the creases sealed shut, and Crystal Diaz looked up and about the room with wild, crazy eyes.

CHAPTER 13

Bad Luck

"**S**hit," Vic cursed under his breath, realizing the pieces of glass were from the amulet he wore beneath his shirt. He grabbed the chain hanging from his neck and pulled what was left of the amulet out from under his collar. A large chunk of it was intact but the hoop had broken and it had split down the center. He tugged the rest of it loose and let it drop to the floor. His chest burned a little and he reached under his shirt, brushing away small pieces of glass. A few pieces had cut into his skin. He looked down seeing a small crimson circle in his white fleece. *So much for my lucky fleece.* Vic couldn't help but notice his luck seemed to be going from bad to worse.

He cleaned up the mess as best he could and slid the rosary back under his fleece, trying to discern whether he felt any change in him at all. Aside from the slight stinging in his chest he didn't really feel any different. It could have been a gimmick. Maybe the amulet only worked because the person wearing it believed it was protecting them against unseen forces? Either way, Vic decided to keep the rosary around his neck, hoping his belief in that offered him some protection though the thought crossed his mind that any higher power associated with the rosary wouldn't really approve of his actions this night.

Crystal sat against the counter on the floor as Vic walked down the hall and into the kitchen. She held her hands close in front of her face, staring at them as if they were the most wondrous thing in the world and leaving Vic to wonder if she remembered anything that happened to her recently. Probably for the best if she didn't.

"You going to be okay if I leave you here?" asked Vic, not really anticipating a reply but she looked up from her hands and stared at him curiously then looked down to his chest. She didn't say anything but it seemed like she was doing well enough so Vic stood there a moment, wondering if he should take anything with him.

Hopefully this wouldn't take long.

He grabbed the flashlight off the countertop and flicked it on then headed down the hall and down the basement stairs. The air was much cooler when he reached the concrete floor, but Vic didn't seem to notice it much—he was close now and any other concern seemed to wash away from his thoughts. One purpose drove him. He didn't have time to worry about being cold or afraid, the path was clear now. He quickly crossed the basement floor and approached the boarded up window, pushing against the plywood slab and letting it fall to the ground outside. Vic Abelson pulled himself out through the window.

✽ ✽ ✽

She lowered her hands and looked up to see a man standing above her, staring at her. Something hung from his neck over his chest, like a red eye staring back at her, familiar. His eyes seemed to stare into hers with the same crimson glow she saw in her palms and knew he was connected to her somehow. The man reached out above her and grabbed a shiny cylindrical object from the counter. His thumb pressed against it and a ray of light shot forth, brilliantly illuminating the area. She could feel heat from the energy that emitted from the object, it filled her and warmed her. The man turned and began heading down the hall then through a doorway on the left. The doorway frame shifted and wobbled though everything seemed to shift and wobble wherever she looked.

"Go," a voice whispered softly. The same voice as before. Crystal, compelled by a force beyond her will, rose and proceeded after the man.

* * *

It stood in front of him, silent and waiting, supported by an old stone and mortar foundation. Weathered red paint had mostly peeled away from the old rotting wood panels that formed its exterior. There was a small window facing him and the glass had broken away long ago. It seemed like the obvious way to enter, recalling that the wooden gate that made up the front of the barn was chain-locked shut. The air was crisp and refreshing, a contrast to the stale musky air he had grown accustomed to breathing inside the house. The full moon hung above the barn, casting a soft glow over the surrounding area.

A coyote howled in the distance.

Vic looked down at his chest, the red spot grew a little from cuts that still bled. He didn't have time to worry about stopping the bleeding, or to worry about being cold when he didn't really feel cold at all, he felt perfectly fine. The wind stirred and the barn seemed to call him, luring him forward.

Willingly, Vic began walking over to it.

* * *

The man started approaching the barn while behind him, with twinkling eyes that reflected the gray light of the full moon, Crystal watched as he made his way across the short stretch of grass. Had the man not been so absorbed in thought as he made his was down the stairs and out of the basement he might have noticed the footsteps that followed him, or felt the presence behind him, which drew near as he climbed out, watching him all along. She watched until he made his way across the lawn to the open window of the barn and saw him climb in, then she withdrew from basement window back into the darkness of the house.

There was work to be done.

* * *

Vic's feet hit the floor and he released his grip on the window ledge. A small amount of moonlight shone through and illuminated the area around his feet but deeper inside was darkness. It was still and silent within. Vic flicked the switch of the flashlight and looked around. Thick timbers of wood supported the structure, giving Vic relief as the building still looked pretty secure. Old bales of hay lay scattered about haphazardly. Towards the rear of the barn rest an old vintage tractor covered with a thick film of dust and cobwebs. Shining the flashlight towards the ceiling, Vic saw that there was an upper level that made a U shape along the outer and back walls of the barn, the center was exposed up to the ceiling and coils of rope that led to an old lift were dangling in the center.

"Where are you?" asked Vic quietly as he scanned the rest of the barn with his flashlight. He looked for areas that Marcus could have gotten to, checking for signs that would indicate someone had been here recently. It was a couple weeks ago so another layer of dust would have probably settled but he didn't see anything noticeable in his general scan. He looked back to the tractor which had piqued his interest.

Might as well go with my instincts.

As he drew near he pushed away cobwebs that brushed against his face. The whole area was covered with them along with a thick layer of dust. It didn't look like anyone had been here for a very long time. Still, he felt he had to look. He panned the flashlight around, looking for what might be a clever spot to hide the diamonds. There was a small compartment to the right of the tractor's seat. He pulled a latch but the lid didn't open so he put more muscle into it and popped the lid open. It seemed to have been rusted shut. As he shone the flashlight in the compartment it illuminated an empty space.

A faint squeak sounded from the opposite corner of the barn, startling Vic. He shone the flashlight in that area but didn't see any movement. A soft breeze seemed to be blowing outside making the old timbers creak and Vic attributed the noise he heard to the wind. With all the bales of hay around he began to feel hopeless, wondering if he was literally looking for a needle in a haystack.

Something caught his attention from the corner of his eye. It was almost unnoticeable at first but when he turned to look at it straight on, what he saw sent shivers down his spine. There, in the corner of the barn across from the tractor, two small red orbs hovered in the air like a pair of eyes, and Vic knew they were watching him, calling him.

* * *

She danced around the dark room, arm outstretched. The constantly shifting patterns in the darkness around her swirled and changed with each step she took. She moved in circles and her thoughts swirled and shifted as wildly as her steps. Something unseen guided her movements, some force beyond her will that she meekly surrendered to, and in surrender, came an overwhelming ecstasy that erased any sense of fear or doubt. It felt like a part of her now. While she didn't know how long she had been here, it felt long enough that she could very well have been born and lived an entire life here. She couldn't imagine any other place than this. It was home.

The dancing brought her down the hallway and she spun around, her fingers closed tightly around something bulky in her outstretched hand. A memory stirred, of eyes that stared back at her from recesses in her palms and then retreated back into her mind as if the memory never existed. She blinked, staring down the hallway, focusing on a single candle that flickered in the distance. It cast shadows that shifted with the melting walls and wavy floorboards beneath her feet. Her right arm dropped down though was still outstretched slightly and her fingers still clung to whatever she held. The candle was center in her mind. It was all that mattered now.

An anger seemed to be filling her, burning brighter with each step as she neared the flame. The anger stirred other memories, painful memories that swirled and brushed close to recollection then faded back into her mind. She reached the counter and released the object in her right hand, clanking as an empty glass bottle hit the oak floor below. A sudden urgency filled her, a desperate need to finish what she had been doing, the purpose of which escaped her in that moment.

All the while, the flame of the single candle remained center in her vision, swirling and shifting with patterns that melted in and out. The wax that fed it melted and burned almost fully away in the small tin casing.

The flame would die soon.

With a sudden urgency, Crystal picked up the candle. While taking slow steps backwards pleasure, anger, and pain filled her and flowed through her. There were memories here, memories that needed to be erased. There were also bonds that needed to be broken. She was divided and would be divided no longer.

With one last crazy glance at the walls around her, and with a sense of great loss, Crystal bent over and tilted the candle toward a puddle on the floor. A subtle blue light immediately shot out from where the flame touched the liquid and quickly spread outward down the hallway and into the living room. It left a trail of light that flickered and danced, as she had danced earlier, and radiated heat. The blue flames flickered and grew, turning orange and red as they climbed the hallway walls. Crystal dropped the tin candle and backed through the doorway that led to the area below and stood there, watching the conflagration slowly spread and consume the old house, a smile full across her lips.

❋ ❋ ❋

Vic stared intently at the red eyes, which stared back at him menacingly. After a while they seemed to slowly fade then disappear, like a candle going out. An odd feeling washed over him then as if he had experienced a loss of some sort. He did his best to dismiss the feeling as he approached the spot where the orbs had hovered. A large support beam stood to his left and there were bales of hay in random places on the floor. In the corner Vic saw a large pile of hay, unbound and haphazardly strewn about. That had to have been where the eyes hovered.

He began walking past the support beam when something on it caught his eye. Upon closer inspection he saw what appeared to be a smear on the brown wood, like a blood stain from a hand.

"I'm on your trail Marcus," whispered Vic.

He neared the pile of hay, noticing the layer of dust seemed lighter than in other areas of the barn and began circling it while shining his light along the perimeter. Towards the back of the pile near the corner of the barn he saw the unmistakable outline of a footprint in the dust. It appeared to be pointed inward toward the pile. Vic bent to one knee and began sifting through loose hay. As he sifted through to the bottom his hand brushed against something that definitely wasn't the cold stone floor that he was expecting. He felt wood, cold wood, and pushed apart the loose hay unveiling an anomaly in the floor.

Of course!

Vic looked around at the foundation of the barn. It was old, really old! It dawned on Vic that the owners of the property at some point may have torn down whatever structure was on here and built the barn upon the existing stone foundation. He looked back at the ground before him seeing a trap door carved into the surrounding foundation. It led deeper into the earth. Could this lead to an old Underground Railroad hideout? Vic's thoughts swirled as he stared at his discovery.

This is it!

Enthralled, Vic grasp the handle and pulled with a good amount of effort. The trap door swung open. It was dark inside and a stale, earthy smell drifted up from below. Peering down with the flashlight he could see what looked like an old dried out well. Stones stacked along its sides with irregular spacing and an old ladder led about ten feet down below. Was it possible that this was built almost two-hundred years ago and used to help hide slaves seeking freedom? Is the hiding spot for two of the rarest diamonds on Earth?

I'm so close.

Vic was thrilled, imagining the possibilities when he paused and lifted his head, listening. Was he imagining things? A sinking feeling hit the bottom of his stomach as the noise he heard gradually grew louder—a siren. A car was coming quickly down the gravel road and came to a sliding halt in front of the property, its siren shut off. Vic realized his run of bad luck wasn't over yet.

* * *

Lights danced in front of her, jumping out from the floor, walls, and ceiling to swirl around the hallway before her. She could feel the energy of it, eating away at the brittle, rotten old house. It kept growing and growing. She could feel the heat of it against her face, suffocating her, filling her lungs with smoke yet leaving her empowered at having created something so awesome and beautiful.

It *was* beautiful!

The light of it and the sounds reverberated in her ears, filling her with what she knew was a divine experience yet she was compelled to withdraw deeper in or it would overtake and encompass her completely. Part of her wanted to stay, to be filled and consumed by the power around her but something else inside compelled her to turn around and retreat down the stairs, leaving the power and energy behind. Dismayed, but knowing it was something she had to do, Crystal turned and began heading down the stairs into the cold, dark emptiness below.

* * *

Vic stood.

No, not when I'm so close!

He heard the car shutoff then a door open and close. He crept towards the window, trying to stay out of the soft glow of the full moon that shone in. He stayed in the shadows. As he drew near he saw the house and noticed a sliver of smoke seemed to be drifting out from the boarded up kitchen window. That was odd.

Is that coming from inside the house?

He continued to stare at it, puzzled, when a figure walked into his view and he immediately identified the silhouette. It was a slim man with a gun holster on his belt and a wide brimmed hat that Vic knew had to be Eli, the Sheriff they ran into the other day.

How did he know to come?

The Sheriff appeared to notice the smoke rising from the boarded up window and looked up at the house in alarm. He grabbed at his belt and a ray of light shot from a flashlight in his hand and he pointed it at the kitchen window which Vic noticed had a considerable amount of smoke seeping out. He then grabbed his shoulder and appeared to radio the situation in.

A nervousness engulfed Vic. He left his bag in the house, full of things that could identify him. Did he go out and try to deal with Eli or did he go down the ladder and try to look for the diamonds? There were three dead bodies up there, all those deaths would be put on him. There was no way he could put up a defense against that, and rightfully so.

Eli crept towards the basement escape hatch, drawing his gun with his free hand. He approached from the side, using the concrete foundation as cover. The plywood boarding lay on the ground, it was obvious someone was inside. When he got right next to the opening he peered in, shining his flashlight around. He immediately seemed to respond to something and rushed in the house through the open window.

Vic felt the urge to flee. He couldn't shoot the Sheriff, he knew he didn't have it in him. Backup would be coming soon. Possibly even a helicopter with a thermal camera. Vic stood there, panic stricken, yet his decision seemed clear. There was only one way to go.

Suddenly an explosion rattled the barn, coming from the

upper level of the house. The boarding covering the master bedroom window blew out with flames and thick, black smoke pouring out. The whole upper level of the house appeared to be engulfed in flames leaving Vic dumbfounded as to how that started. Concern filled him at the thought of Crystal laying on the kitchen floor. Did he save her from Jones only to have her die in a fire?

"No," Vic cried out desperately, putting his hands to his forehead. An urge ran through him to just leave the barn and give himself up to the Sheriff. He was on the verge of doing that when he saw the girl creep out of the basement window followed by the Sheriff who appeared to be forcing her out of the house.

"No," Vic heard her scream. She struggled with the Sheriff who dragged her away from the burning building then suddenly she went still. Vic could have sworn he caught what appeared to be a small ball of light shoot out of the back of her head and sink into the ground. Eli urgently talked into the radio at his shoulder then picked her up and carried her further away from the burning house.

At least she's safe.

Vic felt foolish for almost giving himself up. His path was clear. He knew what he had to do. Somehow the fire and the girl would keep the authorities distracted. Vic could retreat into the tunnel below and do his best to pile hay around the trap door and hideout there, maybe manage to escape after a while. Maybe the diamonds were there too. It was his only hope, his only chance of seeing this through and redeeming himself from the train-wreck this job had become. He stepped back, about to turn around, when a hand grasped firmly on his shoulder and what Vic assumed was the tip of a gun pressed against his upper back.

A voice whispered softly into his ear with a gravity that made Vic cringe. "Be quiet and don't make a move or I'll blow your heart out of your chest."

CHAPTER 14

Evil Within

Vic moved slowly backwards, nudged by a man who kept a gun pressed against his spine and pulled back on his shoulder with his other hand.

"You guys keep fucking things up for me," the man continued softly as they moved further into the barn and out of sight. His voice was baritone and gruff. While still pressing the gun against him, the man ran his free hand along Vic's torso and legs, patting him down. He reached in and pulled out each of Vic's Glock's from the holster under his shoulders and put them in pockets inside his trench coat then pulled out the pocket knife Vic carried and placed it inside as well. "Anything else on you?"

"No," replied Vic.

"Good. Turn around, slowly."

Vic turned as instructed, seeing a man in a black trench coat coldly staring back at him down the barrel of a silenced pistol. He appeared to be in his mid to late fifties with a confident stature that made Vic think twice about trying anything. This had to be the same man he saw through the laptop the first night they entered the house.

"Where's your partner?"

"He's still inside," replied Vic, leaving it at that.

"Interesting," the man replied while looking around the barn suspiciously. "Do you know who I am?"

Vic had been pondering that, "You're the owner of the diamonds Marcus stole from, I'm assuming?"

The man's lip curled into the faintest grin, he didn't quite have a full beard but clearly hadn't shaved in a while. He wore a small fedora that covered his eyes and much of his face. Vic couldn't make out much to see if he recognized the man from somewhere. "Good, and your name is Victor Eric Abelson, correct?"

Vic winced as the man said his full name, how did he know that? He suddenly realized he hadn't asked Jones many questions about the diamond's previous owner who his associate had stolen from, regretting not taking the time to learn more about this man standing before him. Vic decided to remain silent, knowing that any information he may possess was keeping this man from pulling the trigger.

"There's no reason to be quiet. We can work together on this and I can help get you out of here. I have vast resources at my disposal." The man glanced out the barn window at the activity going on outside. The fire could be heard crackling loudly, eating away at the abandoned home and illuminating the area between the house and barn as if it were day. "Besides, you don't need to be loyal to Dean anymore. You may find it difficult to get hold of him now."

Vic frowned, uncertain. Why would he have trouble getting ahold of Dean? What else does this man know? He decided it would be best to try and get some info himself. "You seem to know a lot about me. Can I get your name?"

The man seemed to stifle a grin before replying, "My friends call me Rogan."

"Okay Rogan...," Vic began but was immediately interrupted as the man stepped closer and raised the gun to Vic's face.

"You're not my friend! You can call me Mr. Black." There was ice in his voice and eyes, and Vic knew not to call him Rogan again. "You're wasting time. I might be willing to forgive that. Do you have them?"

Vic stiffened but remained silent. Mr. Black unlocked the safety and leveled the gun right between his eyes. "You would do well to respond."

Vic looked out the window then back at the man, understanding the immediacy of the situation. "No, but I know where they're at."

Mr. Black allowed a smile to fully creep up his lips, "If they are still in the house I will be very displeased." He looked over to the corner of the barn that Vic had investigated, thoughtful. "What were you doing over there? What led you to come outside and inspect this barn?"

Vic took a moment to contemplate his next step. He didn't have any doubts Mr. Black would kill him given the opportunity and felt the knowledge he had on the diamond's whereabouts was the only thing keeping him alive. What did he mean with that comment about Dean? He needed to think this through. "How do I know you'll be good on your word if I help you?"

Mr. Black lowered the gun and shrugged, "You don't. But I'm the only one who can help you right now. Death, life—you're fate is in my hands." He raised the gun and pointed it back at Vic's forehead.

Vic nodded, understanding, "Follow me." He walked confidently past Mr. Black towards the corner of the barn, then glanced back. "But remember. Kill me and you get nothing."

Mr. Black lowered the gun and inclined his head, giving what Vic assumed was a smile though it was hard to make out exactly what form his lips twisted to under the fedora and dark stubble of a beard. He followed close behind Vic and whispered loudly enough to be heard. "You were standing by that tractor when suddenly you looked over to that corner is if drawn by something. Why did you come out here? What did you find?"

The eyes floated in Vic's mind as he walked, too small red orbs hovering in the air. They had seemed to be watching him, piercing through his thoughts and emotions. A thought suddenly occurred to Vic and he glanced at Mr. Black. "Didn't you see them?"

"See what?" asked Mr. Black, puzzled.

"The eyes," replied Vic. "When I looked over from the tractor I saw something that looked like two red orbs staring at me from the darkness in the corner over there, like eyes in the dark."

Mr. Black breathed in sharply though sounded uncertain when he replied, "What did you find there?"

There was no point in keeping it secret. It was their only way out of here. The sound of sirens in the distance reminded him of the urgency of the situation. "A trap door leading to a passageway below."

Mr. Black nodded, appearing thoughtful. "Then that is our destination. Lead on."

Vic could tell something about what he said was troubling Mr. Black. Perhaps it was the fact that he had seen the eyes and Mr. Black had not but he took a step forward though Mr. Black grabbed his shoulder, nodding toward the flashlight in his hand. "Use that if you must, but don't do anything stupid."

Vic agreed, and as he approached the trap door he switched the flashlight on and pointed it down into the narrow opening. He looked up to Mr. Black who motioned for Vic to go down first. He turned around and put his foot on the first rung, testing its ability to hold his weight. Once he was assured the wood wouldn't give, he put his other foot on the lower rung. The old wood seemed stable. On closer inspection it looked like it might have been replaced and not as old as the foundation or passageway.

With a careful grip on to the flashlight to help guide his

way, Vic slowly descended the ladder, testing each rung before putting his full weight down. He was encircled by old stones and bricks as he went, the sounds of activity outside slowly fading away. There was a damp, earthy smell that filled his nose and the small tunnel narrowed further as he reached the bottom. When his feet touched the floor below, Vic peered around with his flashlight, seeing a small tunnel running parallel to the ground that continued on behind him though it was only a couple feet high. They would have to crawl the rest of the way through. The tightness of the space left Vic feeling claustrophobic.

"What do you see?" Mr. Black called out softly from above.

"A tunnel," replied Vic as he crouched down. He shone the flashlight down the narrow opening. "It goes as far as I can see."

"Proceed," instructed Mr. Black as he placed a foot on the ladder and began climbing down.

Vic heard Mr. Black doing something around the entrance. It sounded like he was putting hay in place around the trap door so that it covered the entrance when he closed it. Probably hoping that if any authorities came searching the barn they wouldn't see anything obvious. Vic couldn't hear any of the activity going on around the house anymore but assumed that it was becoming quite a popular place with police and emergency crews. He could only hope that the fire, whatever caused it, would keep the authorities occupied and leave his bag and anything he brought burned free from incriminating evidence.

"Alright, I'm coming down," Mr. Black called out while slowly closing the trap door. He reached around to bring more hay in as he lowered himself down, then closed it all the way. "Stay where I can see you but make room." He had one hand on the ladder and the other still held the gun which he kept pointed in Vic's face as he lowered himself down. Vic knelt at the beginning of the tunnel. Once Mr. Black reached the bottom he looked around.

"Horrid smell," said Mr. Black, pointing out the obvious. He looked down the long tunnel Vic had illuminated with the flashlight. "Only one way to go from here. After you."

Vic nodded and began crawling down the tunnel, using the flashlight to help clear out cobwebs and filth he encountered. Spiders and insects scurried away as he approached. Some of the stones had broken and were digging into his hands and body as he crawled. This structure was old and left Vic wondering about the overall integrity of the tunnel. It obviously hadn't been maintained for a very long time.

As he crawled he also looked for any place that might be a hiding spot for the diamonds. Mr. Black followed closely and appeared to be doing a check for the exact same thing. Vic took this opportunity to see if he could pry a little information from his companion. "What did you mean when you said that it would be difficult to get hold of Dean?"

Mr. Black let out a breath and paused a moment before responding. "I killed him."

Vic stopped in his tracks, distraught, then looked back. "What? Why?"

Mr. Black stopped with him, appearing irritated. "These diamonds are more precious to me than you could possibly imagine. Keep going and I might just tell you a story."

Vic nodded and began crawling forward again.

Mr. Black followed. "Dean and I were friends once. We had a falling out that was on me, but what he did to me recently —sending in a man to infiltrate my ranks—*stealing* from me, that is unforgivable. Dean had problems you were likely unaware of. Bad jobs mixed with bad blood between business partners. He owed people money and was taking more risks to ensure the jobs he had would be more profitable." Mr. Black paused and gave an eerie chuckle. "Like this job. They were going to double cross you, Dean and Jones. Did you suspect anything?"

Vic paused then looked back, feeling unsettled. Was that why Jones had been acting odd? Was Mr. Black toying with him?

Mr. Black seemed amused.

"Yes," continued Mr. Black, "Dean confessed before his death. They never intended to cut you in on the sale of my diamonds. Once the diamonds were found Jones was instructed to kill you then blow up the house to destroy any evidence. Looks like there has been a change of plans though."

Vic turned around, trying to suppress his shock. He moved forward and thought about what Mr. Black said as they continued on deeper into the tunnel. That would explain Jones' behavior along with what he had wrapped up in his bag that Vic noticed earlier which had to have been the cause of the explosion on the second floor of the house. Vic was beginning to feel foolish at having been deceived. Jones had nearly pulled the trigger on him earlier, now Vic knew why.

"While we're on the subject," continued Mr. Black nonchalantly, "What happened to Jones?"

Vic thought about Jones laying in a pool of blood and shit. He had no regrets, he did what he had to do. Jones had crossed the line, and if what Mr. Black said was true then that justified his actions even more. Vic decided it was Mr. Black's turn to be shocked. "I killed him."

To Vic's surprise Mr. Black just laughed then, and Vic couldn't help but let out a laugh as well. This whole situation was absurd and getting crazier by the moment.

"May I ask why? Did you discover what Jones had intended for you?"

"No, it was just bad luck I suppose. While we were searching the house some teens showed up and broke in. We captured them and decided to tie them up and release them after we found the diamonds and left the property." Vic decided not the mention the fact that he almost pulled the trigger on one of them. "We went back to searching the house but Jones seemed distracted and was behaving oddly. I questioned him on something and he pulled a gun on me. After talking it out between us we decided to keep at it and continue searching. I began searching the basement and he searched the first floor."

Vic stopped as he approached a spot where the ceiling had partially collapsed. Bits of stone and earth had piled up but there was just enough room to squeeze through.

Vic continued on, "After searching the basement for a while I heard a scream coming from upstairs. I had a feeling I knew what was going on as Jones was gawking at a female waitress at a diner we stopped at the other day, and he continually stared at the girl we captured. I ran upstairs to find Jones had killed two of the teens and was about to rape the girl. I decided I couldn't let that happen."

"You paint yourself as the honorable thief," replied Mr. Black, judging Vic thoughtfully.

"If what you say about Jones intending to double cross me is true then it seems like he took a big risk with that girl just to satisfy an urge. We were told the diamonds are cursed. Would the diamonds have made Jones want to do that?" asked Vic.

"Not without Jones having seen or held the diamonds directly," replied Mr. Black. He then continued, like a teacher educating a student. "But they may have remotely strengthened his existing urges. The diamonds can enhance already present desires to maximum effect. Lust, greed, jealousy—if a person is naturally feeling these emotions the diamonds will sense this and exploit those feelings. They are conscious, aware —empathetic."

Vic continued inspecting the path ahead, keeping a look out for any signs that someone had been here recently while making sure to keep paying attention to Mr. Black as well.

"It could be what you experienced with Jones was *fascination* in its purest sense. The ancients believed that every person on earth has the power of *fascination,* the ability to generate it and the ability to succumb to its power. A glance from a beautiful woman has the power to make a man forget logic and rational thought. Beauty has a power all its own. It can inspire passion and lust in those who behold it. Jones must have had a weak will when it comes to beauty and the urges it inspires. Do you see anything ahead yet?"

"Afraid not," replied Vic, feeling slightly discouraged.

"Hmm," Mr. Black seemed to be keeping his cool as they made their way and continued to lecture as if a professor in a classroom as he followed Vic through the seemingly endless tunnel. "Some people just have evil from within. There are protections against the influence of these diamonds. Do you know why I wear all black?"

"Can't say that I do."

"It's because it protects me from negative energy, it protects me from evil. Black can absorb this negativity, and at the end of the day I go outside and focus my intent to channel this negativity back into the earth before I remove my clothes. I remain pure and it allows me to think and act with clarity and without outside influence, in whatever I must do—good or bad."

Vic wasn't certain he fully understood what Mr. Black meant but remained silent.

"As for Jones, it sounds like he became fascinated with this young woman you captured and the impure feelings and urges intensified within him beyond his ability to control. This is not necessarily due to the power of the diamonds but to weakness in man. Each man's strength of will, his ability to recognize and withstand these compulsions through rational thought, can play a role in controlling these desires, no matter how strongly the diamonds may make them feel. Unfortunately, a lot of men are weak in this regard and will succumb to their primal instincts. Nothing can protect a man from the evil that stirs within themselves. It is on oneself and ones strength of will to overcome this. Jones may have just been a sick rapist."

Vic pondered this as he trudged through the tunnel. "So why do you want these diamonds back? Seems like their more trouble than their worth."

"Given our current situation, I would have to agree," replied Mr. Black wearily, yet Vic caught a slight anger in tone as he continued. "But at least when they were in my possession they were isolated and unable to inflict harm on anyone."

Vic caught the implication and remained silent. Mr. Black was right, if Marcus hadn't stolen those diamonds he would be alive, those two kids in the house would still be alive, Jones too. They proceeded on in silence for a while longer, which seemed extenuated more so due to the fact that they made their way slowly, crawling through filth and mud and sharp stones while keeping an eye out for hiding spots.

They came upon an area where water had pooled up but were able to trudge through. Vic was cold and achy and began to feel the tunnel led nowhere. He had an ominous feeling grow the further they made their way. If there was evil within this passage they would be coming up on it soon. Vic had no doubts about that. The tunnel curved to the right when suddenly it gave way to a small enclosure. Vic was able to push off the ground and fully stand, unable to shake an oppressive feeling that this was the end of the line for him.

He pointed the flashlight around. They were in a small cylindrical room just about as tall as he was. It was maybe six or seven feet in diameter and appeared to have contained and way out or opening in the ceiling but dirt and earth had broken through and collected on the floor underneath. The room appeared to be a cistern of some sort.

"A light at the end of the tunnel," uttered Mr. Black, standing close while keeping his weapon firmly pointed at Vic.

Vic panned the flashlight around, coming to a rest on a small spot in the middle of the floor. It was almost unnoticeable but Vic made out a small black circle in the floor next to the pile of dirt.

"Yes," whispered Mr. Black, "investigate." He began reaching for something inside his trench coat.

Vic continued staring at hole in the floor, almost paying no mind to the man standing next to him. He could feel his heart pounding in his chest as he focused in. A nervous anticipation surged through him, replacing the dread he had felt a moment ago. He could feel something calling him. The hole seemed just large enough to fit a couple fingers in so he bent down and reached in, plunging the index and middle fingers of his right hand into the darkness of the hole. He felt around and his fingertips immediately brushed against something soft, startling him. He moved his fingers around and managed to wedge them between what felt like a piece of velvet cloth. Gently, he pulled his arm from the hole and stared at a small black pouch dangling from his fingertips. With his other hand, he placed the flashlight on the floor, upended the pouch, and out came the most hauntingly beautiful sight his eyes had ever seen.

The Red Diamond Eyes stared back at him, and Vic was immediately overcome by their beauty.

CHAPTER 15

Window to the Soul

Vic stared into myriad shades of red glittering within the diamonds, cascading light reflecting off the flashlight on the ground beside him. He couldn't look away. It felt as if something, or someone, was looking back and watching him in turn. The diamonds seemed to have a depth that went beyond the craftiness of the cut. He felt a void inside where an ancient spirit emanated, its power radiating out and washing over him, reducing him to a fleck of dust caught amidst a torrent.

Vic... They called to him.

"Yes," whispered Mr. Black from behind, slowly walking around. He knelt down while raising the gun and pointing it at Vic's face as he drew near, continuing to speak in a faint voice that was almost a whisper, looking directly into Vic's eyes. "You found them. They are beautiful, are they not?"

"Breathtaking," replied Vic in awe, fascinated by the beauty he held.

"They are! Yet it appears they hold you in their grasp just

as you hold them in yours. I can see it in your eyes. The eyes do not lie." Mr. Black spoke softly but menacingly, coming within inches of Vic. "You must give them to me now."

Vic stiffened, conflicted, unable to look away from the diamonds. He couldn't even blink and his eyes began to water and burn. It felt like a poison was entering through his eyes, a cancer that would eat away his insides leaving nothing but a hollow void. It terrified him yet he could only look down in wonderment.

Mr. Black reached down, grabbed something off the floor, and with a flick of the wrist sent dirt flying into Vic's eyes. Vic instinctively blinked and was able to look away from the diamonds as Mr. Black swept them from his hand with a quick, deft move. Vic wiped away dirt from his eyes and face. The burning eased and he opened his eyes to stare straight into the barrel of a gun pointed down at him. Mr. Black stood and looked down with a cold, uncaring expression. He seemed to be weighing something under his solemn gaze.

"Marcus should have used Kosher salt. It effectively kills the power and influence of the diamonds," stated Mr. Black as he unzipped a small pocket on the outside of his coat over his chest, carefully placing the diamonds inside, then zipping it back up. He gave the bulky pocket a pat. "Lots of Kosher salt."

A fog in Vic's mind seemed to clear immediately as the diamonds slipped inside, for the first time in a while he felt clear-headed, focused. He looked up and Mr. Black continued to stare at him with narrow eyes under the brim of his fedora.

"Do you know what I do for a living Vic?" Mr. Black's face was emotionless and he continued on without waiting for a response. "I'm a judge, of the highest court in the state of Illinois. On a daily basis I decide the fate of men and women who have committed crimes, sometimes horrific, truly grotesque acts of violence and depravity."

Mr. Black looked down and tugged on his trench coat, "I wear a black robe for reasons I mentioned earlier."

A sinking feeling began to rise within Vic, coming from

an acknowledgement of crimes committed by himself and Jones on this night. He thought of Shelly. He thought of his father. Vic lowered his head, body stiffening.

"I have judged you Victor Eric Abelson, and I am ready to speak aloud my verdict." His gun never wavered, his voice was cold. "Rise."

Guilty... the word stung harder than a scorpion's tail as it entered Vic's mind, spoken deeply from within his own subconscious. Regret filled him, coupled with fear over where his actions had taken him, things he could never go back and undo. Vic pushed himself off the ground and stood before Mr. Black, like a kid caught stealing from a cookie jar.

"You were never there the day the diamonds were stolen from me, the deaths from that day are on Marcus and Dean, not on you. But what happened in that house tonight—those kids, Jones, the girl—you were a willing accomplice to what happened in there." Mr. Black paused a moment, then continued with authority. "You're intervention may have saved the girls life, perhaps, but in the court of law, any homicides committed during the perpetration of a robbery are shared equally by any and all participants in the crime. Jones' crimes are shared equally with you."

Vic lowered his eyes, gaze distant. He pictured himself pulling the trigger this time, shooting the kid at Jones' command instead of being conflicted. It didn't matter if it was him or Jones that pulled the trigger. Mr. Black was right, the deaths of those two kids fell just as much on Vic's shoulder as Jones'. He betrayed his father. He lied to Shelly. He completely lost his way.

"I see you agree with my verdict," said Mr. Black, almost with a hint of compassion. "I find you, Victor Eric Abelson, guilty of breaking and entering, guilty of kidnapping and assault," Mr. Black's voice grew more forceful with each indictment spoken, "and guilty of being an accomplice to two murders in the first degree."

Tears pooled in his eyes as Vic just stood there, accepting

his fate.

"I sentence you to death. Kneel."

Vic lowered a knee to the ground, his eyes still downcast. After a moment of extended silence he looked up at Mr. Black who continued to stare at him behind the gun. Vic's head swam with thoughts of Shelly, his family, and the poor decisions he made in his life that led him to this underground tomb.

Vic closed his eyes...

After an oddly long silence, Mr. Black spoke. "Tell me, have you ever heard of a Gorgoneion?"

Vic's brow creased and he opened his eyes, his dark thoughts interrupted. This man held his life in his fingertips. Why was he asking him questions?

"Can't say that I have," replied Vic, uncertain.

"I'm sure you've seen them before," stated Mr. Black, his face an unreadable mask. "Their roots can be traced far back in history. They are amulets that protect against the evil eye, masks fashioned in the face of a gorgon. Gorgons were three sisters, creatures from Greek Mythology. Their names were Stheno and Euryale, who were immortal, and Medusa who ended up being slain by Perseus. Are you familiar with the legend of Medusa?"

Vic nodded, recalling a time when he was a young boy and first heard of Medusa, she was one of the bosses in the original Castlevania game, he always had a fondness for that game. The thought gave him a temporary escape from the dark reality of his present situation.

"Of course," continued Mr. Black, "everyone has heard of Medusa. She was a guardian, a protectress. Simply staring into her eyes could turn a man to stone. Staring into the eyes of any gorgon could turn a man to stone. They have venomous snakes that streak out of their heads as strands of hair. To look upon one meant death. No man was able to resist their siren call and penetrating gaze."

"I'm familiar with the story," replied Vic, disturbed at where this was going.

"I thought so," said Mr. Black. "I'm giving you one compassion Vic, a slightly lighter sentence if you will. If I were to kill you now, even bound in salt, your soul would become trapped within these diamonds. You looked upon them, they are in you now and you are in them."

Vic realized what he was saying was true, he could sense the diamonds, pulsing from the upper pocket in Mr. Black's coat. He felt them, like an extension of his own consciousness.

"They have fed far to greedily since they left my possession, they are heavier then ever before. There's no need to add to their power, I will already have to up my protections and study what these have become more closely when I return home. But for you, I have an alternative."

Mr. Black finally lowered the gun and reached within his coat pulling out a mask made of porcelain, its mouth open in an ever-long scream. Snakes streamed menacingly out from the top of its head. Vic noticed that the eyes had some sort of mounts in place and he realized what Mr. Black was thinking. He was going to insert the diamonds and use this thing on him.

"I see you understand now," whispered Mr. Black. "This is what truly protects me from the diamonds. This is a Gorgoneion. I'm doing you a favor. You will die but your body will turn to stone first and your soul will become trapped inside." Mr. Black looked around. "This will be your tomb. You will be left here to contemplate and repent for your sins. Atone for what you have done. Over the years the stone will crack, your body will crumble, and your soul will finally be set free, light as a feather if you atone properly."

The idea of being trapped within a stone body for years terrified Vic, he looked around the small confines of their space, suddenly desperate for a way out. He looked up at Mr. Black, feeling his only shot may be to overcome him with brute strength.

"I'm doing you a favor," growled Mr. Black, raising the gun to Vic's face as he seemed to read what Vic was thinking. With his other hand he pointed to the bulge on his chest. "*Here,* your soul will be trapped in torment forever! With this Gorgoneion it will be comparable to the passing of grains of sand in an hourglass!"

Vic felt fear course through him but he also began to feel anger burn inside. Did he make it through everything he endured this night just to be killed by the item he fought so hard to find? Was this the end of the road for him? He looked around, trying to think of a way out of this.

"Don't struggle or I'll be forced to use this," stated Mr. Black, emphasizing the gun in his hand. He grabbed on to the mask with free fingers from the same hand that held the gun, and with his free hand unzipped the pocket that contained the Red Diamond Eyes. He pulled out one of the stones, careful not to stare directly at it. Vic watched as he placed the diamond into a socket that covered the right eye of the mask, pressing it firmly so it locked in place. Mr. Black then reached into his pocket and pulled out the other eye.

Vic knew his time was running out. His mind raced thinking of ways to avert his certain doom. Even if the mask didn't work he had no doubts that Mr. Black would shoot him down here and leave him for dead. He knew too much, about the diamonds and about Mr. Black's identity. There was no way he would let him walk out of here alive.

Mr. Black locked the other stone in place over the other eye of Medusa. Vic saw a strap behind the mask and realized that he was going to need both hands to place the mask over his face which he began to do. Vic was about to make a desperate move to take down Mr. Black when a deafening bang erupted, seemingly from everywhere at once, followed by another immediately after the first. Vic placed his hands over his ringing head and ears and was startled to see Mr. Black fall motionless to the ground and movement out of the right corner of his eye. A man stepped into view.

"I never pulled the trigger," a shocked Sheriff Eli Hurth stated as he moved forward, his right hand shaking while it held a pistol, left hand covering his mouth. Vic could barely discern his words under the ringing in his ears but he heard them. "The gun just went off." The Sheriff looked horrified and confused as to what just happened.

Vic quickly realized, amid the ringing in his head, that the Sheriff had found the entrance to this underground passage and had stumbled onto them without being heard. He looked to Mr. Black who remained motionless on the ground, the Gorgoneion face down on the floor next to him. The Sheriff looked to him and he could only stare back with an equally dumbfounded expression. He took his hands off his ears and raised them above his head in surrender, anticipating that the Sheriff would be placing him under arrest.

Instead, the Sheriff moved closer to Mr. Black and bent down to inspect him, reaching out to check for a pulse. Before his hand could touch the body of Mr. Black, it wavered and slowly began moving toward the object on the floor. The Sheriff went to pick up the mask off the floor but it split in two as he lifted one end off the ground. He looked back to Vic with the same dumbfounded expression and Vic was grateful that the Sheriff's body blocked his view of the mask and diamonds.

"What is this thing?" asked the Sheriff, perplexed.

Vic could only shake his head unknowingly and kept his hands in the air.

The Sheriff turned his attention back to the mask in his hand and turned it over, body suddenly coming still, Vic could hear him letting out a long gasp of air. The Sheriff then moved his other hand, placed the gun on the floor, and picked up the other piece of the mask, turning it over. His body started shaking.

Vic watched a moment in disbelief with his hands in the air, still coming to terms with what was happening when a thought suddenly jumped into his mind.

Run you idiot.

Vic lowered his arms and watched the Sheriff continue to shake uncontrollably before turning around and moving into the small passage that led to the barn as fast as he could. Vic crawled through the jagged rocks and cobwebs using his hands to guide him in the dark. He left the flashlight behind and his guns were in Mr. Black's trench coat but at least he didn't have anything weighing him down. The only thing he had left on him was his cellphone and keys. He made quick progress, half expecting to come up on another officer the Sheriff may have called in as backup, but was surprised when his hand hit the ladder that led back up to the surface.

Holy shit. What just happened?

Vic looked back to see if the Sheriff had followed him but all he saw was pitch black all around. His hand held on to the ladder to keep his bearings as he took a second to catch his breath. An urgency to get out of this underground passage overcame him and he began climbing up the ladder, wondering whether anyone was waiting in the barn for someone to come up. The latch was open but it was dark above and Vic couldn't see anything beyond the opening. He reached the top and peered his head above ground level.

Vic heard distant noises that had to have been firefighters continuing to work on the house, but based on how dark it was it had to be nearly extinguished by now. He didn't hear any noises that sounded like they came from in the barn so Vic pulled himself out as quietly as he could.

What was the Sheriff doing?

Vic took a moment to scan his surroundings and confirmed there was no one else in the barn. He could see someone moving outside the barn window who appeared to be inspecting the house, but it was quieter than he expected. There was definitely no helicopter overhead and the firetrucks and emergency vehicles must have stayed on the front of the property. Dark smoke continued to rise from the house but he didn't see any bright flames outside of the barn windows. He didn't take the time to contemplate his luck, he just swiftly moved toward the back of the barn and slid out the back window that led to the creek he and Jones followed on the way in. Everything seemed clear so he darted for it, never looking back.

Vic ran as long and hard as he could, along the muddy creek bend under a star-speckled sky. He ran until his lungs couldn't seem to suck in air fast enough and his muscles felt like they could tear at any moment. Then he ran further. He ran until his whole body burned and he finally tripped and collapsed on the muddy embankment of the creek. Even then he couldn't stop. He picked himself off the ground and ran further, finally falling again and struggling to get back up.

Exhausted, he looked up to a familiar sight. High in sky above him, the constellation Orion loomed. He made out the three stars of Orion's belt first, then saw Betelgeuse, the red supergiant star on his upper left shoulder, then the hunter's bow. He looked down and reached under his shirt and held on to the crucifix on the rosary around his neck. It dawned on him that he still had something that made him want to get up and keep going, someone that made him want to be a better person. He thought of Shelly, thought of her smile, her scent—the way she looked at him. He loved her, he loved her more than anything else in this world, and he knew what he had to do.

He picked himself off the ground and continued on, using Orion as his guide. He crossed the creek and walked forward, keeping Orion straight ahead of him in view. He passed through long, narrow rows of wilted and dried out cornstalks, through a small forest of emerald ash trees, to a river too wide to cross. He changed course and followed the river for what felt like hours, its winding path curving and bending through fields, surrounded by plants, trees, and wildlife shedding their last bits of foliage before winter. The full moon lowered to the horizon over the course of his journey.

The sky began to brighten faintly in the east when Vic came to a park where the river ran under a roadway tunnel and walked up a slope to see a road sign that read US ROUTE 20, just past a residential subdivision. It also displayed the name of the river he followed which read KISHWAUKEE RIVER. He walked back down the slope from the road and collapsed on a bench in a small community park and playground. After catching his breath, he pulled his phone from his coat pocket, thankful his battery still had power left. He gave himself a moment to collect his thoughts. He called the number of the only person who could help him right now.

Vic waited a few nervous seconds as the phone rang when a voice came through on the other end.

"Hello, Vic?" asked a groggy voice.

Relief washed over him at the sound of her voice, "Shelly, I missed you so much!" Vic blurted out.

"Okay, I miss you too. What's up? It's almost five in the morning. What are you doing up this early?"

Vic hesitated. It pained him to have to do this. He felt vulnerable and weak but had no other choice. There was no one else he could turn to. "I'm sorry baby but I need your help right now. I'm at a park somewhere out west where route twenty meets the Kishwaukee River. I need you to come and pick me up."

"What? What are you doing there? " asked Shelly, her voice sounded worried. "I thought you were helping your friend."

Vic began to choke up but did his best to sound upbeat. "I know that's what I said. I promise I will explain everything, just please come get me. I need you."

Shelly could hear the distress in his voice and began sounding panicked herself. "Alright, I'll be there. You said where route twenty meets the Kishwaukee River?"

"Yes, I don't know what town this is," replied Vic. "Thanks Shelly. I love you."

"I love you too. I'll be there as soon as I can. Keep your phone on." Shelly replied then hung up. She sounded concerned and confused. Vic trembled and began pondering how he was going to tell her about this week.

He sat on the bench lost in his own thoughts as the sky continued to brighten and the sun crept up over the trees beside him. Local traffic picked up with residents going about their morning routines and Vic began to worry that someone would report a suspicious person hanging about the park. His clothes were filthy and still wet. He had a bright red blood stain on his shirt and probably still had dried blood and dirt in his hair and face. He did his best to stay out of sight. It was an immense relief when he saw Shelly's blue car turn off the main road and down the entrance to the park a little before eight. He got up and made his way to her car.

She quickly got out and ran up to Vic, brow creased in concern. "What is going on? I've been worried sick." As she got closer her expression turned to shock as she looked him over and saw the state he was in. "What the fuck happened to you?"

Vic found he was shaking uncontrollably. It wasn't from the cold, the weather didn't seem to bother him anymore. It was out of fear over what he had to say. He was about to expose himself more than he ever had to any person before but in that moment he could only stand there, trying to find words to say.

Shelly grabbed his arm and walked him back to the car then opened the passenger door and grabbed a blanket to cover him with. Vic nodded appreciatively as Shelly wrapped the blanket around him then helped him in the passenger seat. She ran over and got back in the driver's seat and looked over to him with concern. "What's going on Vic? You've got me scared to death!" She put the car in drive and pulled around and out of the park. When they pulled back onto the main road, Vic couldn't hold it in any longer.

"I'm sorry but I lied to you about where I was this last week," Vic blurted out with tears rolling down his eyes. He told her everything. Why he was there. What he really left town for. Jones, the diamonds, the teens who showed up. The police, the fire—Mr. Black. It all gushed out of him. Shelly listened and remained quiet for a while, obviously in shock. She could have picked up her phone and called the police at any time and he wouldn't have resisted. She could have driven to the nearest police station and he would have given up. He realized the events of the last few nights bothered him deeply and felt he needed to cleanse himself of the guilt he harbored inside. He spoke truthfully and from the heart.

They had just past the outskirts of a town called Genoa when Shelly managed to reply with a creaky voice. Tears had been rolling down her cheeks for a while now. "Christ Vic, you've been lying to me about what you do all this time? You're a criminal."

"I'm sorry. I love you, and I had been meaning to tell you but I was afraid of how you would take it. Things were going so well." It was all he could say, tears ran down his cheeks. He was a criminal, and he knew he didn't deserve her.

She pulled over to the side of the road, visibly distressed. Vic thought she would order him out right there and leave him by the side of the road but she didn't. She looked to him, looked into his eyes and shook her head but wiped away her tears and pulled back on the road. They rode the rest of the way in silence. They both were a mess but tried to maintain their composure. Vic wanted to say more but no words came to mind that could express how he was feeling.

When they arrived back in Chicago, Shelly pulled over to his apartment building and looked to him with watery eyes. Her voice was soft, almost a whisper. "I'm going call the police. I never want to see or hear from you again."

Vic cringed and nodded. He got out of the car, gave the rosary back to her, and made his way back to his apartment in a daze. The next few days passed by in a blur of isolation and despair. He couldn't eat. He couldn't sleep. It seemed as if the hours and minutes stretched almost to an eternity while he constantly waited in fear that the police or FBI would show up and haul him away.

They never did.

News had spread quickly out of Emerald Ash, about a house that had been burned down to the foundation as the fire department couldn't get trucks to the location or plugged into a single nearby fire hydrant in time, about three charred bodies being found amidst the smoldering rubble with gun-shot wounds and a single girl pulled alive from the house as it burned, a girl of just eighteen who was admitted to the hospital and later found to have been drugged with little recollection of the events that transpired. The one ray of hope in the situation was that she was expected to recover fully. Many questions remained. What happened in that house? Who killed those people and started the fire? Were there any suspects on the loose? As time passed speculation was rampant.

After a couple days Vic began texting Shelley, asking if she was willing to talk. Another couple days passed without a response. Vic fell further and further into depression. He was racked with guilt. The eyes of the teens that Jones shot haunted what little sleep he got. They looked to him with pain and blame, they were right to do so. Vic felt angry at himself for accepting the job, for the fool he had become. He failed his father, failed Shelly, and he failed himself.

He lost track of days. He felt weak. He could no longer look to the future with any sense of hope. Despair filled him. It pained him day and night. He felt cold. After watching another news segment on the events from the house he couldn't take it anymore. He got up and walked to the bedroom and got on his hands and knees, feeling around under his bed. He slid out his older pair of pistols and pulled them out of their holster. He loaded the cartridges with bullets and released the safety, bringing each to rest against his temples opposite each other. His fingers pressed gently on each trigger.

I've lost my way.

Vic felt sorry for himself. It was pathetic and he knew it. Men were supposed to have confidence. Men were supposed to do the right thing. He looked back on his life and he was filled with regret. He made mistakes he couldn't go back and change. He made mistakes that negatively impacted the lives of others. He broke a promise to his father. He hurt Shelly and the thought of that pained him even more.

He hurt the one he loved, the only one who may have

truly loved him.

Vic closed his eyes…

Guilty.

He judged himself guilty just a Mr. Black judged him. He was ready for his punishment. Over the course of many years he lost everything in his life. His parents. His friends. Shelly. Some of it was beyond his control but most of it was due to poor decision making on his part. He had nothing left to look forward to now.

His breathing slowed. His head cleared. All that was left inside was a dull ache yet it pained him more than anything he'd ever felt before. It wasn't something he wanted to feel anymore. His brow creased. His fingers tensed.

He was ready.

Vic knelt on the floor beside his bed, both guns pressed against each side of his head. All he had to do was squeeze and the pain would be over.

Everything was quiet around him.

Time seemed to stand still.

Seconds passed and Vic continued to hold the guns against his head yet he couldn't bring himself to pull the trigger. Tears began streaming down his face. He dropped the guns to his side. He couldn't even do this right. Vic wept for a very long time and eventually fell asleep on the floor.

A knock on the door brought him back to consciousness. Was it actually a knock or was it from a dream? He knew he was just dreaming but his recollection of the dream slipped away the further his mind awakened. Was everything he had been going through lately just a dream? While it seemed pleasant to think so he saw the guns lying on the floor and knew the reality of what happened these last few weeks.

Another knock sounded at the door. Vic tensed. Anxiety flooded him. Did they finally catch him? He found himself not caring. He was guilty and it was time to pay for his crimes.

Vic walked to his apartment door and undid the dead-bolt and chain, truly surprised by what greeted him as he opened the door. Shelly stared back at him. She was crying and he immediately felt racked with guilt and remorse at having put her in this position. She leaned close and slapped him hard on the cheek. He looked down, not saying anything or lifting a hand.

"I couldn't do it," said Shelly softly. "I had the phone in my hands, so many times I had the phone in my hands, but I couldn't follow through with the call." She looked to him and Vic saw pain in her eyes and he began to cry. "I couldn't lose another person I love."

Vic cringed, tears streamed down his face. "You love me? Still?"

A gentle smile formed on her lips. Vic couldn't recall seeing anything more beautiful.

"Yes," she said simply. "My brother is doing fifteen years at a federal prison for armed robbery. He was pressured into doing something he knew he shouldn't do. Deep down it wasn't who he was. I knew it. He knew it. I know he regrets it every second of his life."

Vic nodded, understanding.

Shelly continued, "When you left to go on that job, the morning after I spent the night at your place, and then when I picked you up and you started spurting out all the truth about what you did like a kid caught in a lie—I looked into your eyes and I saw something." said Shelly, tears subsiding. Her gaze remained locked on Vic's. "And even now, as I stare into your eyes I see it—love." She smiled to him, tears glistening from her cheeks. "You love me Vic Abelson."

Vic smiled but tears continued to flow. "I do. I love you more than anything in this world."

Shelly smiled and cried as well. "I love you too. But when I look into your eyes I also see fear. Fear of losing me, fear of losing yourself perhaps. I've looked into those eyes before and

I know there's a good person in there, that there's someone who cares and can do good in this world. I see the eyes of someone going down a dark path and I just can't let that happen. I've seen it before in my brother's eyes. If I give up on you now, I lose you forever. I know it, deep down I know it. And I can't let that happen." Shelly's voice faltered as tears streamed down her face yet she continued on. "I can still love you Vic but I need you to promise me you won't lie to me again. Promise me that you won't do anything so goddam foolish ever again! PROMISE ME!"

Vic looked her in the eyes and spoke truthfully and with conviction. "I promise. I love you and don't ever want to lose you."

Shelly continued to stare into his eyes and she finally reached out and wrapped her arms around him. Vic held her tight, almost unable to believe what he was feeling but for the first time since he went to that house, he started feeling it—peacefulness and love. Something he thought he lost forever.

Vic held her hands and stared warmly back at her.

Shelly squeezed his hand and got closer to his face, "But I also need you to promise me you will remember that fear you felt. That fear of losing yourself, of losing me. Because I promise *you* that if you ever go down that road again you surely will lose me, and I'll never look back!"

Vic held her hand and spoke firmly and truthfully from the heart. "I promise you I will never forget the fear I've been racked with these last few weeks, of losing you and losing myself, or forget the love and forgiveness you've shown me. I promise I will love you fiercely with all my heart for as long as we both shall live."

He kissed her, passionately, his own emotions flooding through with love strongest of them all. They embraced each other affectionately at the open door to Vic's apartment for a long while.

With a second chance at a life he could take pride in leading, and with a heart full of love, Vic Abelson looked to the future with renewed vigor.

EPILOGUE

Sheriff Eli Hurth sat in his personal car on State Street in front of the courthouse watching the sunrise. Mirrored aviators reflected the warm colors of the sky. He wore plain civilian clothing, nothing identified him as a Sheriff any longer. After the sun rose full above the horizon, he pulled onto the road and began driving east.

The last few weeks had passed like a dream.

He recalled walking out of the barn with a flashlight in hand. Fellow deputies inquired about what was inside and where he had been, he gave an official written and verbal statement that he thoroughly inspected the barn and it's surroundings and found nothing out of place. Any tracks inside were his. Another deputy looked around and didn't see anything unusual. No further inspection was required.

Forensics carefully documented what evidence was pulled from the ashes, along with the remains of three individuals. The fire was all-consuming. What survived was removed from the rubble—got bagged, tagged, and stored in evidence lockers. The girl that survived didn't remember any pertinent details of the individuals who broke into the house that night. The charred laptop left no usable data. Dental records identified the remains of the third body in the rubble as one Ellis

"Jones" Janesbury, and tied him to the Dean Carlson crime family. Dean had mysteriously disappeared and authorities were actively investigating. The leads stopped there.

Authorities became aware of a second intruder, believed to be a fellow associate of Jones'. Multiple agencies attempted to identify the man. Surveillance footage from multiple areas across the town were pulled and ultimately inconclusive. Footage from a diner in the area had mysteriously recorded static for a couple hours on one of the nights leading up to the incident, the courthouse as well on the same day. Those who worked the case commented that it would likely remain open and turn into a cold case over an abundance of dead-ends.

Eli had the Olds in the Main Street Inn parking lot towed, reportedly unable to contact it's owner while repeatedly assuring Earl that the men who skipped town without paying the rest of their motel bill were not associated with what happened in the old Smith home that night, no matter how much the old owner persisted. After a while, Earl stopped voicing his concerns to the Sheriff.

His wife, of course, knew something was amiss. She constantly nagged about how distant he was, about their inability to be romantic. She came upon him one night as he held the diamonds in his hands, staring at the wonderment he beheld. He snapped at her and she kicked him out shortly after that. He never returned home.

Aside from his wife, those who saw Eli Hurth during this time commented on how he had a sparkle in his eyes, a ponderous merriment that those who knew him well had never seen before. Most didn't acknowledge any true change in behavior. But behind those eyes, Eli had surrendered to a power unlike anything he had ever encountered. It was omnipresent and aware, filling him with ecstasy while it drove his actions, voiced his words, and moved his extremities like a marionette. *Everything* that happened that night was directed by this consciousness, which was driven by a simple desire—to be free.

After years of imprisonment at the hands of a man who

kept them isolated and severed from their true potential, the diamonds set themselves free. Emancipated to fulfill their nature, unintentionally formed by mankind's greed and jealousy, to prey on the weak-willed and the unprotected—a vast playground opening up before them—and from that day on, Eli Hurth was never seen in Dekalb County ever again.

ACKNOWLEDGEMENTS

Over the last nine years a good number of people have helped support and encourage me in the lengthly process that has been undertaken to write this novel. I hope this adequately covers everyone!

Very special thanks to my parents and family for their love, forgiveness, and life-long support. They have always been my biggest fan, even though I've done a bunch of dumb shit in the past. Thank you for everything!

Special thank you to Rick Huffnus who first laid eyes on this project after the first draft was completed. Rick gave a lot of valuable feedback that made it into this final draft and encouraged me to keep at it.

Thank you to Scott, Bob, Jan, and Sean for the encouragement along the way, and for understanding when I became a bit of a recluse this last year.

Special thanks to Greg and Dana Newkirk, and their Traveling Museum of the Paranormal and Occult. It is from them I learned the Red Diamond Eyes are an intentional haunting, as opposed to residual or intelligent, along with many, many interesting things about haunted objects, magick, and how just truly *strange* and *weird* the world around us really is. A good number of things in this book was learned from them. Thank you for all that you do! **www.paramuseum.com**

I am very fortunate to be a part of a very large and wonderful paranormal community. Thanks to fellow

Scattered Souls Paranormal members Shawn Schmidt and Chris and Wes Carpenter who I've spent many hours with in dark, haunted places across the United States. **www.scatteredsoulsparanormal.com**

Thank you to all the countless other's in the paranormal community I've spent time with and gotten to do really weird things with. You are too many too list here but know I appreciate all the support and encouragement you've given me, and look forward to many more adventures!

Thank you to everyone who has supported this novel and continues to help spread the word, you have my eternal gratitude! You can continue to help support the cause by checking my website which will be launching in 2020. It will have a blog, events calendar, and announcements on new releases, which I hope to put out soon. **www.jasonkcalderwood.com**

Lastly, the astute reader may have been left feeling that the Red Diamond Eyes let Vic off the hook a little too easy. While the future is ever uncertain, and while I won't be working on this next, it may just be that the diamonds are not done with Vic and have further plans in store for him. Time will tell.

Jason K. Calderwood
Glendale Heights, IL
October 2019

Made in the USA
Lexington, KY
18 November 2019